CROSSING THE GREAT DIVIDE

Crossing the Great Divide

A Collection of Short Stories

Nancy Roberts

WIND PUBLICATIONS

First edition

International Standard Book Number 1893239381
Library of Congress Control Number 2004114265

ACKNOWLEDGMENTS

The author thanks the editors of the magazines where these stories, some in slightly different form, were originally published:

Alaska Quarterly Review — "The Importance of Birds," reprinted in *Telling Stories: Fiction by Kentucky Feminists*
American Literary Review — "Cornbelt Blues"
Ascent — "Sea Change"
Beloit Fiction Journal — "Color Blind"
Beloit Fiction Journal — "Wichita"
Confrontation — "Angel's Landing," reprinted in *Open 24 Hours*
Crosscurrents — "City Electric"
Explorations '93 — "Cold Hands"
The Gettysburg Review — "Another Garden Party"
Journal of Kentucky Studies — "The Great Barrier Reef"
MidAmerican Review — "Pete's Rock"
Open 24 Hours — "Under the Tornado"
Ploughshares — "Blood of the Lamb"
South Dakota Review — "Dear Lily"

Grateful acknowledgment for support and funding is given to The Wichita State University, the University of Illinois Research Board, the Ucross Foundation, and Western Kentucky University.

Nancy Roberts' photo by Doug Keese, used with permission.

This one is for Shane
And for my brother Craig

In memory of Lisa and Fern

I cannot rest from travel; I will drink
Life to the lees. All times I have enjoyed
Greatly, have suffered greatly, both with those
That loved me, and alone;

— *Ulysses*, Lord Tennyson

The birds teach me how to fly home.

— *Refuge*, Terry Tempest Williams

TABLE OF CONTENTS

City Electric

City Electric wasn't working out, and Drew was afraid to tell her husband. Everyone knows you can't blame the horse. A few quirks in temperament will complicate things, but whatever a horse does, it's been taught, whether on purpose or by mistake.

So every day she saddled up City Electric and started over. First there was the walk, the gait you must establish if you want a horse you can ride. Drew knew it was no use trying to hold her back, for a horse is stronger than a person. What you need is quietness, so Drew would croon to her, stroke her neck, keep the reins relaxed. The horse would walk a few steps, then, as if some motor had switched on, begin jigging, trying always to go faster. Cantering, the horse would swing her hindquarters to the side, trying to force a gallop. At a gallop, Drew knew, this horse would drop to its knees before it quit, so it was no use trying to wear her down. At the end of the ride, the mare's beautiful dark coat would be streaked with creamy lather. New blisters would have come up on Drew's fingers, and she would be discouraged.

She took lessons from the trainer at the barn, who stood with his legs apart and finally lost patience. "Why can't you do what I ask?" he said. "You can make her mind!" Drew could not make her mind, though daily she tried.

City Electric could bounce over jumps like a little ball, tight and smooth, the higher the better. But at shows she flattened out like a snake, flung her head into the air, and crashed blindly through the jumps or ran right past them in a frenzy of speed. Once the mare jumped clear out of the show arena, just missing the corner of the announcer's stand.

After that her trainer said, "Give up, she's crazy." But Drew wiped her arm across her sweaty forehead, said, "There must be something I'm doing to irritate her. She's very sensitive."

When she'd go home, Barry, if he weren't away on a business trip, would glare at her. Before they'd moved out West, and even for a while after that, he'd been a man who bounced on his feet when he talked to her. He used to be so eager to share his thoughts he'd tumble a bright wash of words over her like a joyous river. She'd laugh and finally have to say, "Slow down!" So much abundance gave her the luxury of being caught by him and swirled about. And she'd get to be the one who said, "Enough!" But he'd grown resentful of something, perhaps of her time with City. He withdrew himself like a hooded bird, seemed every day to be more distant.

One day she decided to be brave and have it out with him. She walked up to the TV, which was always on these days, switched it off, and said, "We've got to talk."

"My game is on," he said, "Move, please." He aimed the remote control at the screen and waited for her to move aside.

"Then when?" she said. "You choose the time."

"Later. Please. My game."

Later, she knelt next to him on the bed. Her hair, grown long and permed to please him, was brushed into a foam of curls. She said, "Come back."

He looked up at her from the book he was reading and said, "I haven't gone anywhere."

He had green eyes that sometimes looked dark. His eyebrows grew together in the middle above the high bridge of his nose, making him look perplexed, which was a thing she loved about him. "Oh, but you have gone somewhere," she said. "I want to bring you back!" She touched the place where his brows met, then bent over him so that her hair swept onto his chest.

He sat up a little, and his eyes darkened. He seemed to be remembering something and then forcing himself to be angry. Anger from him used to be a wonderful thing. He'd fuss and growl about some small oversight, and then hook an arm around her, say,

"Sometimes I love you so much I can hardly stand it." Who could mind an anger like that? But now the anger was a studied thing, as if he were pushing himself away from her for a certain reason. The effort was costing him. His lovely vividness all held inside, he seemed strangely lost and sad.

Drew sat up and pulled her hair over her bare breasts, suddenly embarrassed at her nakedness. She got up, put on a robe, sat down on the edge of the bed. "Please," she said. "Can we talk about it?"

"About what?"

"Is it about the time I spend with City? Would you like to come with me sometimes?" When he didn't answer, she swallowed hard, and said, "I'm sorry I haven't done better with her. I want to make you proud of us."

He sighed, smiled a little and squeezed her hand. "Nothing's bothering me."

"Do you miss New York? Was it a mistake to move out here?"

"I can't talk now. Let's sleep."

She could not sleep, so she went downstairs to her studio, a place where she could forget about herself. She took out a ball of wet clay, pummeled it, pressed it flat, mounded it back up. Then she sat with her hands cupped around the lump of clay and waited for it to tell her what to do. But clay seemed to have run out of things to say. She wondered if sculpting is like what they say about lyric poetry: it pours out for a few years and then the gift is gone. Training a horse is a kind of sculpture, she thought, pure fluid form and power, freed and shaped within the frame that you create. But with City, the power ebbed out of her hands like water. The horse would not enter the partnership you need for art. It was a matter, she resolved, of finding the right approach.

Because everyone knows a horse's attitude is improved by trail rides, she rode City into the foothills. As she picked her way down a steep sandy slope, City noticed something, a bird perhaps, and leaped sideways, nearly lost her footing. On the next trail ride, they came to a little ditch, which the mare decided she didn't want to cross. She bucked and reared and ran backwards. Then from a standstill she took a sudden leap at the ditch, clearing it by several feet. Headed home, she shied violently at rocks and parked cars she'd passed calmly on the way out, hoping perhaps to unseat her rider. And always she refused to walk. Drew came home from these trail rides unable to think clearly about her life.

Perhaps what Barry resented was the expense. She wasn't getting anywhere with her sculpting, ought to go back to work, maybe do some paste-ups for an ad agency in town, a newspaper. Even a little typing would be fun. She missed the sense of purpose a job gave her and the easy companionship of an office. But he'd said he didn't want her to work, so she decided not to ask him about this.

She stayed home and watched a game with him, thinking she'd been selfish always doing what she wanted. She made popcorn, brought him glasses of beer. He permitted her small services and was intent on the game. Her presence didn't seem to matter much. Well, she shouldn't mind. She was, after all, entering his world, so it should be on his terms. The hard thing was that she did not want to be there. She wanted to cover her ears against the announcer, whose frenetic voice seemed to insinuate itself into the very depths of her being. The intricacies of the plays were spoiled by all that piling up and crashing into.

There had to be a better way, some neutral place where they could meet and find their marriage again. She suggested that they hike together, but he said he didn't think he had the energy. This was odd, for in New York City where they'd met, he'd walk from Gramercy Park to her apartment in Yorkville, a good sixty blocks. It must be hard, she thought, to relax into the expanse of the western landscape when you'd lived all your life by city lights. Although she'd lived by those same lights, coming to the mountains was coming home for her. For him, it was as if something inside him had gone out, and she did not know how to help him.

Sensibly, she took her next trail ride with a group. This particular ride involved many water crossings. At an especially daunting ford, the horses in front walked carefully across the rocky stream and scrambled up the steep bank of muddy clay on the other side. In her eagerness to catch up with the other horses, City tried to jump the whole thing, landed on the vertical upslope, clinging to the treacherous wet clay like a spider on a wall. Drew flung her arms around the horse's neck, and somehow stayed aboard while the mare heaved herself up the rest of the bank. Drew's lip was bleeding from the sudden crush of her face against the horse's crest; she thought her nose was broken. She had to ask the group to wait while she collected her breath and stopped trembling. She gingerly pressed the bridge of her nose. Everyone there told her it was a spectacular jump and also that her horse was sort of crazy.

She told Barry about her little adventure. As she touched her swollen lip, she longed for a bit of sympathy, though she knew she didn't deserve it. It was her fault, having such a fine horse and not being clever enough to train it properly. Perhaps it was too late for her to have a horse.

She remembered the dreams about horses she'd had all through her teens and twenties, when a real horse was out of the question. She'd think the dreams had actually happened; they were so vivid. Sometimes she'd be at a show, ready to ride, and along would come her father, saying, "No. You have to come home right now." Or she would have lost her boots, her cap, or couldn't locate her horse. Then, at last, when she was almost thirty, she dreamed that a white horse came to her window in the night and she finally got to ride. She twined her fingers into his flowing mane and the two of them soared bareback over hedges, gardens of night-blooming flowers, rooftops, wide moonlit rivers.

Barry made it all come true. There weren't many men in this world who would pay for lessons in Central Park, and then for a horse when it became clear that she had become a serious rider. He'd been proud of her in those early days before they were married, would come to watch her show the school horses, had even helped out a little with grooming and fetching water. And then, as a wedding gift, he presented her with City Electric, a dark bay thoroughbred whose eyes glinted like polished obsidian. Everyone said, what a catch Barry was: well-to-do, women wild for him, generous besides. She and Barry left the city soon after to move out west, for he'd decided to do university computer research, and was no longer tied to New York. Living in the West was her dream, she'd told him, and he'd been eager to please her. They hired a van to ship the horse, and out here the horse had become almost her entire life. She had only a few tenuous friendships, as new friendships always are, but what did it matter if she had a husband and a horse?

"Thank you, God," she said every morning—though she was not sure whether she still believed in God—"for letting me have a horse." This made up for having been born a woman, which she knew her husband, if he were religious, would every morning thank God he had not been born. His father had been a rabbi from Germany. Perhaps as a consequence, Barry disliked all things religious, and was thoroughly American, which was probably why he liked football so much.

The TV tube burned out. She was filled with hope. But he rented a set while his was in the shop, going to all this trouble with the air of someone who would not be daunted. At breakfast, she tried this:

"Barry?"

He looked up at her over the newspaper, his eyes soft and green from sleep.

"I'd like to have a baby." It had occurred to her that perhaps this was the great thing missing from their life together. Men, after all, marry to have children, and here she'd been running off to the barn like she was a child herself. It was time to grow up, to be a person who gives.

"You would?" He set down the paper and rubbed his eyes. He was silent for a moment, and then shook his head. "No. I don't think so. Not now."

"What do you mean, not now? Because of what?"

He looked startled and said, "Oh, I meant not now as opposed to later. I meant, I guess, that this isn't a good time."

"No, this isn't my idea of a good time either," and she laughed, hoping she'd made a little joke. But then: "Why do you seem so sad these days?"

"Who's sad?" he said. He smiled at her and bent back to the paper.

She felt a sudden surge of anger, slapped her hand on the news-paper and pressed it to the table. "Talk to me! You don't notice me anymore. If I didn't know better, I'd think there was someone else."

He was silent for a moment. Then he raised his eyes in which there was more than sadness, almost grief, and he said, "Please."

And so it seemed constructive to leave Barry alone for a while and turn her attentions to City, who was, she'd decided, bored and in need of a challenge. She saddled her up and headed her toward the scree slope of a mountain. The trail curved up the mountain in a series of steep switchbacks and was nothing more than a narrow ledge on a dense fall of pebbles that had broken off from the peak and worn themselves smooth. The slope fell sharply away from the ledge, and as they climbed, the height became dizzying.

Drew faced resolutely ahead, needing to be brave. City stopped a few times, turned her head to gaze up at her rider as if to say, "Are you crazy?" But Drew pressed onward. City coped with this as she always coped with the unknown, by flinging up her head and charging ahead. She slipped and fell to her knees; then she lost her footing altogether and began to slide down the mountain. Drew leaped off and, by the grace of adrenaline, kept hold of the reins, braced herself on the little ledge, and pulled with all her might. City scrambled wildly, sending sparks off the pebbles that slid from under her hooves. Finally she regained her foothold on the ledge. The mare stood momentarily subdued, her legs splayed out, her head drooping. Drew forced herself to get back on. She decided they'd gone high enough. On the way down City didn't miss a step, and Drew wondered if there was such a thing as a horse being too intelligent.

Drew was badly shaken from this adventure. She felt she had run out of constructive things to try with both her horse and her husband. She could no longer face going down to the basement to confront the obdurate clay. This intolerable state of affairs began to tell on her. She had a minor accident in her car at a stop sign, failing to notice that the car in front of her had stopped a second time for a better look. It got so that every time she cooked vegetables she burned them. Sometimes she had nightmares. She woke up at three a.m. weeping. Her husband also woke up and he did not gather her into his arms, which worried her still more. She took long, hot baths, trying to calm herself enough to think. She thought of talking about all this with her new friend, Susan, or even Margaret, though Margaret had troubles of her own. She thought of calling her parents in New York. But she couldn't find the words to make sense of it to someone else.

Now Drew spent her time at the barn driving City round and round on the lunge line, or just leading her with a halter and leadline, letting the horse graze at will. She didn't want to ride for a while.

Barry went on another business trip to New York, where he stayed for a week. Then he phoned her to say he was going to fly to Chicago and check out some new prospects in central Illinois and would be gone another week. There was nothing unusual in this, but when he returned, Drew followed him around the house from room to room, feeling that if she let him out of her sight, she might lose him entirely. All weekend she sat with him in front of the TV, not watching it, but staring straight ahead, hoping he would give her some sign—perhaps a look, a touch of the hand. Before they went to bed, she said, "What's wrong?" But he shook his head, said, "I'm awfully tired."

A new trainer came to the barn. She saw City Electric cantering around on the lunge line with beautiful flowing strides and told Drew she wanted to buy her.

Drew stopped the mare and led her over to the woman, who had the strong, confident face good riders often have. Drew said, "She's difficult. She does crazy things." She lifted her eyes to the woman's and sighed. "But with a better rider, who knows?"

"I don't want her for riding," the trainer said, "I want to breed her to a warmblood. They're calm, might mix well with her talent."

Drew wished she'd thought of that. She felt very tired. And then she felt a great emptiness as she wondered what she would do with her days without City Electric.

The woman looked closely at Drew and said, "There's nothing much wrong with your riding. I watched you at that show. You did a great job staying with her." And then she told Drew about another horse, an Appaloosa experienced on mountain trails, built right for jumping, who'd been abandoned by his owners and could be had for very little money. An Appaloosa? Kid's horse, cow horse. But yes, she agreed to go look at the horse, whose registered name was Cherokee Bill.

Bill was almost white, with a few black spots on his rump. He was smaller than City, a disappointment when you're looking for a jumper, and his whiteness was a shock after City's wet-dark sleekness. But then he turned and looked at her with the kindest eyes she had ever seen.

Though he'd been trained for a western saddle, she put her lightweight jumping saddle on him, and cautiously mounted, expecting him to sidle away from her the way City did. He stood still. She got on, squeezed a little with her legs. He walked, kept on walking. He trotted when she asked, cantered in a nice slow rhythm, speeded up when she asked him to, slowed down when she pressed her hips into the saddle a little. He came back to a walk, kept on walking. She dropped the reins and still he walked. She found herself smiling. Could something so hard turn out to be this simple?

Drew was afraid to tell Barry she was selling City. After all, she'd been his wedding gift to her. But when she finally told him, he smiled and said, "I'm glad. She wasn't good for you."

She was astonished, gratified, though later she wondered why he hadn't said that about City long ago. So many of her efforts with that horse had been to please him. Then she saw she should have known it really didn't matter to him now.

Bill caught onto jumping as if he'd done it all his life, and soon Drew was riding him in shows, winning ribbons sometimes. She invited her new friend Susan to watch her ride in a show, and Susan stood at the rail and cheered them on. Drew learned that Susan was good person to talk to, and found out, in turn, that Susan had confusions of her own and a wonderful taste for adventure. Drew cut off her long curls, which were forever getting tangled, and got a stylish blunt cut that made her feel incisive and brave enough to go back to the clay, which now seemed to quiver when she cupped her hands around it as if it were gathering up the energy to speak again. She rekindled the hot inner light of independence and sent out an application to attend an artists' retreat in Wyoming.

Bill was a delight on the trail, eager to go, but always sensible. He reached for the bit and curved his strong neck into an arc like a statue. He moved as if he understood everything about her.

There was a glow in Drew's eyes when she came home. She sang as she cooked, found some TV shows she enjoyed watching with Barry, took to wearing pretty nightgowns and brushing her blade of hair until it shone. Barry stared at her through all this. "He's noticing me," she thought. "Someday soon we'll talk, make love."

One evening soon he walked into the kitchen when he came home instead of going directly to the TV. "I want to talk to you," he said.

She turned off the fire under the green beans and followed him into the living room. He sat her down on the sofa.

"I need to know something," he said. His voice was harsh. Again she had the odd thought that he was trying, for some reason, to be angry in that unnatural new way.

"Yes?" She wanted to be glad that he was finally going to talk, but she felt wary, unsure of him.

He drew his brows into a hard line, seemed to be working himself up still more.

"Yes?"

His fixed his eyes on hers and said, "Are you having an affair?"

Drew started to laugh. But the anger in his eyes looked almost real. For one fleeting instant she was confused, wondered if she *was* having an affair. Then she shook herself a little, took his hand, and spread it across the top of hers.

"No, my dear, I am not having an affair. Unless you count Bill."

His face reddened. "Bill?"

"Silly. Bill's my new horse, remember?"

He was silent a moment, then said, "How can you be so happy if you're not having an affair?"

She laughed. "You mean, how could living with you possibly make me happy? Well, to tell you the truth, the way you've been lately, that's not a bad question." She was filled with hope at being able to say this to him and his caring enough to worry about such a thing. From this might be born the new marriage everyone says you can create if you labor long enough. She felt something electric course through her, connect with his hand. She stared at his hand: the veins, the little hairs, the moons at the base of his fingernails. She was lost in the miracle of his hand.

So it was a surprise when she looked up and saw that his eyes were neither green nor dark, but merely cold. It occurred to her then to wonder why he would want to think she was having an affair. Then she saw that he had hoped for a different answer from her altogether. He did not look the least bit relieved, but had hunched his shoulders and was frowning as if facing now another sort of problem.

She pulled her hand out from under his and held it to her chest. She was not ready to think about this. She would not give up so easily. She could be wrong. If you weren't hasty, there might come the great comfort of finding out that you have simply misunderstood. Or, if it turned out you were right, there would be in that, too, a strange and considerable relief.

Blood of the Lamb

The Bighorns float above the haze to the west of our ranch like marble palaces in a fairy tale. Until the woman came, we'd never been up in those mountains. My father kept us to work day after day, or else there was school, and, until the woman, he'd said he couldn't leave the ranch for that long, especially not at lambing time.

My father always knows when the lambs are coming. Some years they come early, when the snow slaps into your face like a horse's tail. Then some of them die. Sometimes they come late and the house gets heavy with our waiting. This year the ewes were on time. All the snow was gone, except on the Bighorn Mountains, which are always covered with snow.

When my mother died a few years ago, Ben was just starting to talk and I got him all worked up over going up into the Bighorns. It gave us something to want. We begged and begged my father, but he kept us busy and he wasn't talking much.

I take good care of Ben: fold his clothes and put them away, draw his bath, watch over him when my father is working the ranch or down to Bucky's. I do most of the cooking. When I put on lipstick and nail polish my father doesn't mind, even though my mother would have said I'm still too young. Every night I roll up my hair in curlers just the way my mother used to. At first I missed her so bad I had to press a pillow against my stomach in order to sleep. Sometimes now, I can't quite remember what she looked like.

The three-wheeler turned over on my father last summer. He was chasing the cows into the close-in pasture, and he broke his leg in three places. He limps now, and I can hear him at night moving around the kitchen when he can't sleep. The uneven sound of it makes me sad. He was out there a long time before the haying men found him. When the men carried him in, he had passed out from the pain and I thought at first he was dead. In the front room we have a sofa. Above it is a picture of Jesus that shimmers rays of light when you move to the side of it. They laid him down underneath Jesus until a neighbor came in a station wagon to take him to the hospital in Sheridan. He came to while we were waiting and he squeezed my hand and said, "Little Mother."

His hair is black and falls over his eyes. I like to push it back and then run my fingers down to his scratchy chin. I like the red dust on his shoulders, the cuffs of his jeans that trap little pieces of hay. I like everything about him

Maybe once a week my father drives us down Route 6 to Bucky's and buys us sandwiches that Bucky keeps in a freezer and heats in a microwave. My father drinks beer, sometimes plays pool. Kids roll around under the pool table, getting in the way of the game. Dogs wander in and out. Neighbor women stop in on their way home from jobs in Sheridan. We know everyone there, except for the out-of-town truckers, and the Arties. The Arties don't belong here. They come from out of state to stay at the fancy white barn across from Bucky's. In this barn they paint pictures or build things out of pieces of junk they find lying around. Once a couple of them made a life-sized bull out of rusty barbed wire. These people come across the road to Bucky's, ask questions about cows and rattlesnakes, and after a few weeks one batch leaves, another comes. I don't like them much. Sometimes my father goes alone to Bucky's when it's too late for Ben to be up and about. This year he went to Bucky's at night more than he usually does, right up to lambing time, which made me nervous. But I shouldn't have worried. He always knows when the lambs are coming.

And sure enough, when the time came, he banged on our bedroom doors. "It's time," he called. The clock said five-thirty. We'd been ready for this for a few days. Ben and I stumbled out of our rooms, fetched the buckets, the bundle of clean rags, and a piece of rope, climbed into the pickup. The sound of the sharp red stones under the wheels seemed to crack the quiet dark night wide open. We didn't need to speak. Before my mother got sick, she'd be with us, with a thermos of hot coffee and blankets to help us stay warm.

The ewes were in the corral where my father had penned them a few days ago. They lay on the ground, most of them, in no particular way, the unborn lambs mounding up their bellies like piles of dirty snow. The shape of them was all you could see in the darkness. Their eyes would be too dumb to tell you much anyway. A few lambs already born bleated for their mothers.

My father moved from one ewe to the other, lifting their tails, feeling their bellies, pushing down when he thought it would help. When a lamb came out, he lifted it into the air by its hind feet to make sure it was breathing. Held up like that, newborn lambs look like wet chickens ready for the pot. Ben and I knew what to do. We tipped the water buckets for the ewes to sip. We patted the rubbery long lambs with rags to dry them.

The sun burst over the ridge, sudden and white, scattering flecks of light across the jagged hills like salt, stinging our eyes. We looked up from what we were doing and blinked at each other as if we'd just noticed where we were. All the lambs had gotten born with no trouble, except for one. The ewe named Sally would not lie down. She paced around and made silly baas like she didn't want to do the job.

My father stood up, leaned over to rub his bad leg and said, "Let's go home. We'll come back later for Sally. I think she's just a slow one." But his eyes looked worried, and I knew there would be trouble. The lamb might be turned around. Sometimes when that happens he has to pull the lamb apart inside its mother. I set the rope down just outside the corral, ready for later, and we went home to eat breakfast.

As we were finishing the last of the eggs I'd scrambled, a car drove up. I looked out the window and saw a Volkswagen, which you almost never see around here. The driver was a woman. "You'd better tell her to come another day," I said to my father.

He pushed aside his plate, stood up quickly, went to the sink, ran the water, slicked some into his hair. "I asked her to come."

Ben began to whine. I didn't know why. I wanted to slap him.

My father was at the door and in came this woman wearing jeans and a clean red shirt. Her hair was cut in bangs and was shorter in the back than in the front, straight and very shiny. She was thin, a little flat. Though she was at least as old as my father, she was kind of pretty.

"This is Drew," my father said. Ben jumped out of his chair and ran over to her. I wanted to yank him away.

"Drew?" I said, wrinkling my nose, "That's very funny. You must be one of those Arties." My father frowned at me. I took a deep breath, offered the woman a chair, and said, "Have some coffee. I made it myself. I always make the coffee."

Then I took the woman on a tour of the house, led her by the hand from room to room. When she saw the picture of Jesus above the sofa, she smiled a little, then put the back of her hand to her mouth to cover it.

The four of us squeezed into the pickup. I had to sit with my feet around the stick. Ben sat on the woman's lap, and after a little while he leaned into her as if he'd known this lap his whole life. I expected this woman to chatter the way Arties do, but she was quiet, staring ahead at the long hills of sagebrush. She looked sort of sad. She began patting Ben's shoulder, absently, lightly, as if she'd done this before. My father looked at the hand out of the corner of his eye, then he looked quickly at the woman's face, quickly away.

The sheep pen was filled with the noise of the mothers baaing deep in their throats and the squeaky lost bleats of the half-day lambs. The animals wandered around foolishly, calling, staring past one another as if they'd given up hope of finding who they belonged with.

"Don't they know who their mothers are?" the woman said.

"They'll sort themselves out," my father said, which was not the truth. He'd match them up later. Sally stood at the end of the corral, her sides bulging like sacks of flour. She was panting. She ran away from my father when he walked toward her, so he had to chase her around the corral to get her down. Even with his limp, he's fast. Her dumb eyes rolled back as he wrestled her to the ground. "Hold her," he said.

I stood back some, waiting to see what this woman would do. She gave a little sigh, then knelt into the red dust beside the ewe. She pulled Sally's head onto her lap, stroked it like it was a cat and made little sounds in her throat.

My father lay on the ground behind the ewe and shoved his arm up inside her. When the ewe tried to get away, the woman pressed herself across its neck, her face nearly into the dirty fleece. Into Sally's ear she said, "Poor Mom. There, there," as if that would help.

"Its legs are caught," my father said. He drew his arm slowly out of the ewe. It was covered with water and blood.

"You'll have to tear it up," Ben said. "I hate this." He spun away from us, started chasing the lambs.

My father looked across the ewe at the woman. He said, "I didn't ask you to come here for *this*."

The woman nodded and gave a scared-looking smile. "It's all right." She stared at his bloody arm. The two of them stared at each other for a long time. Finally, he shook himself a little and said to me, "Go get the rope. I'm going to try to pull it out."

Ben was holding a lamb under its forelegs, dragging its hind feet in the dust. When he saw me go for the rope, he dropped the lamb and ran over to us. "I hate it when you use the rope," he said. But he squatted down to watch.

My father reached back inside Sally and the woman closed her eyes as if she was praying. "I've found its head," he said at last. He took the rope from me, tied a loop in it, and pushed it up into the ewe. It was hard work and his face turned red. Finally he pulled out his arm and handed the end of the rope to me. "When I count three, we'll both pull." He looked down at the woman, who was still sprawled across Sally. "Hold her tight now. Grab her there, by the shoulders." The woman breathed in deep and hitched both her arms around the sheep.

Ben rocked back on his heels. "Hope you don't break its neck," he said.

They pulled. The woman was stronger than she looked and held tight. Sally groaned and bulged her eyes. "Again," he said to me. "Harder." Then the lamb slipped out. My father lifted the loop off its neck, jerked open the lamb's mouth and scooped out a gob of blood and mucous. Then he put his mouth to the lamb's, breathed into it, breathed again. "Live," he said. "Goddamn you, live." It seemed like everything he ever cared about was being poured into this one limp oversized lamb.

After a while he scowled and flung the lamb down, embarrassed by all that fussing. "It's breathing," he said. "Let's go." He looked down at Sally, who was still lying down, her sides sucked in hollow now and drenched in sweat. "She'll either take him or she won't—if she lives." The woman rolled away from the ewe and got up slowly, as if she'd been in a deep sleep.

When we got back to the house, I asked the woman to ride with me on the three-wheeler down to throw hay to the horses. I could see she would rather not. She looked sort of pale. But I made it seem like it would hurt my feelings if she didn't. "Not too fast, please," she said. I looked right at her and said in my mother-voice, "I'm a responsible person. My father depends on me."

"There's no place to hang on," she said.

"Hang onto me," I said. I saw that she was staring at my father with the same look as when she saw his bloody arm. She wanted to be with him, not go off with me. Well, she would have to wait a little longer.

Ben ran up to us and grabbed hold of the woman's leg. "Take us to the Bighorns," he said. The woman started to say something, but I said, "Our dad's going to take us." Ben began to whine. He grabbed higher on the woman's leg and tried to pull himself up to her lap. "I think that would be dangerous," the woman said and tried to stop him with her hands. She looked worried, kept pushing against the wheeler with her feet to find a place to rest them.

My father stepped forward and lifted Ben into his arms. Ben was crying loudly. Huge tears spurted outward from his eyes. I jammed my foot down on the throttle, gunned the engine to its fiercest pitch. The woman flung her arms around my waist. I smiled, let the motor settle, then drove slowly to the horse pasture, careful to miss the rocks, the gullies and dips, the clumps of sagebrush.

I knew that in the slow time of late afternoon when this woman had gone, my father would take us back to the sheep pen. He would match up the lambs with their rightful mothers and put each family together in separate pens at the edge of the corral. And if Sally wouldn't take the lamb or if she died, we'd get to carry it home and feed it.

17

The woman came back the next day. Such a nice woman, wanting to give Ben and me what we'd begged for all those years. She said, "I'll take you to the Bighorns." And then my father said, "Great idea. We'll take the truck. More room for our gear." I would have to straddle the stick again. Suddenly my father had all the time in the world to leave the ranch and do what he would not do just for his own kids, no matter how they'd begged. He called a neighbor to come feed the animals, look in on the lambs. Why hadn't he thought of that long ago?

But yes, it was exciting to see the mountains coming closer and then to be inside them, to see the cliffs soaring up, the road curving into the bright sky, the sheer dizzy drops. When we were just about as high as you could get, not long before we stopped to camp, we drove past a place called Medicine Wheel. Like a schoolteacher, the woman explained that Medicine Wheel was a sacred site that used to belong to the Indians. People said you could feel the good spirits when you went near it. "Be very quiet," she said. "See if you don't feel different all of a sudden." Then she and my father turned to each other. A look went between them as if they were the only ones there. "You felt it?" she said in a kind of whisper. My father nodded slowly, looked embarrassed. "Felt what?" Ben cried, and bounced on her lap. "What? What?" I pretended I hadn't heard.

Ben and I had to sleep in the back of the truck. My father slept in our tent with the woman. When we set up camp, this woman pulled the sleeping bags out of the stuffsacks and spread them into the tent like she owned it. In the morning she came out of the tent wearing a blue bathrobe and smiling more than was right. She cooked pancakes in our frying pan over the fire and even made the coffee. After breakfast, it was her idea to walk around the lake.

So we walked, not saying much. The peaks jutted up around the lake like a giant's ring of fire stones. We climbed over slabs of pale granite that tilted like old sidewalks, sloshed through the fat snow crystals of spring-melt, rotting leaves, deadfall. The sun on the water flashed like the bottoms of a million leaves, and the air was so sweet you wanted to gulp it down like water. I remember it like a movie I wish I hadn't seen yet.

We walked for a long time and Ben was tired. Back at camp we ate hotdogs roasted on green sticks. Then my father and the woman went off for a walk by themselves, leaving me and Ben alone in the campsite. Ben climbed into the cab of the truck and fell asleep. I thought of taking a swim, but then I'd ruin my curls. Instead, I filled a pan with water from the lake, doused the campfire though it was already out, just for something to do. I spread the wet ashes around some with a stick, wondered if my father had remembered to lock up the three-wheeler in the barn, wondered if Sally had died from the hard birth of her lamb.

When we drove out of the Bighorns, my father's eyes were sad. A heavy silence weighed us all down, even Ben, who curled up on the woman's lap, not wiggling as he usually did. It seemed to take a long time to get home, and when we did, the woman gave Ben a long hug. Then she ran her hand down my father's arm as if it was a piece of velvet. I stood back some, so to me, she simply said, "Good-bye." Then she drove away in her Volkswagen and never came back.

Ben cried when my father said she probably wasn't going to see us again, cried many times again in the days afterwards. My father was no help. He spent hours out by the pond throwing rocks into the water. I had to remind him that there were the horses to be fed, hay bales to be bucked, the lambs to be checked.

Everything is almost normal again. The days are coming in hot even before the sun is over the ridge. The horses stay in the shade by the pond, their heads drooping down. Sally is all right, and her big lamb gambols along with the others, never knowing how close it came to being torn apart inside its mother.

There's no haze today and the Bighorns seem almost close. I wish we hadn't already gone to them. It was something I wanted for so long and now it's over, and never will there be a first time with just my father and Ben. The woman who took us to the Bighorns was nice enough, but no one should replace our rightful mother. I'm glad she went away.

I set my saddle on the fence by the back door and begin to walk to the pasture to fetch my horse. How good it feels to ride a horse! I love knowing I can control something that can pound the rocks into dust and explode the smell of sage into my hair. Today I want to ride so bad, I can feel the electricity in my legs. But the phone rings, and because my father depends on me, I run inside the house to answer it.

"This is Drew," says the voice.

"Who?" I'd forgotten her name, but it's her voice all right. She says her name again, says she's calling long distance and she asks to speak to my father.

I feel afraid all of a sudden, as if now everything in my hands could fall apart like weathered sandstone, and so I am glad I can honestly say, "He's to the lambs."

She doesn't say anything for a minute, then, "How are you? How's Ben?"

I say to her, "I haven't got time to talk right now." I want to ride my horse, ride him right now, over to where the lambs are and see if my father needs help. Ben is visiting our aunt in Sheridan. Sometimes it's a relief to have him gone. My aunt wanted me to visit, too, but I know my father needs me here. He depends on me. If something changed that, what would happen to me?

Another silence, and, "Could you ask him to call me? I'll give you my new number."

"I haven't got a pencil," I tell her.

"Could you find one? Please?"

I put down the receiver, look for a pencil but can't find one. Even so, I pick up the receiver and say, "All right."

The woman tells me the number twice, loudly and slowly as if I'm deaf or stupid, makes me say it back to her. "Be sure to tell him," she says. "It's important." I write the number on the table with my finger and say, as if I'm in a dream and not myself at all, "Yeah, I got it."

The woman says a nice good-bye and hangs up. I fill a thermos with lemonade and go outside. The heat floods into my face as I feel the shame of my lie, but already the sun is spreading little heat-lakes of light across the pasture, the red rock bleeds into the sagebrush, and I know my father will be glad I've come.

Another Garden Party

First there's the context, which, for the sake of the obvious is, say, a large backyard. You could widen this context—the neighborhood, the city, the universe—and see how the meaning of the yard changes, not to mention the meaning of the party. And so much depends upon the reader, so to speak.

Peter, who is the "reader" in this case, is not unreasonable. He views this party through only a few of the possible lenses. Okay. The party is in a backyard consisting of a lawn framed by trees and some late-blooming roses. In the distance, the mountains. Take away the lawn, there's no meaning in the placement of the trees and flowers, and without those there'd be no tension, no edge. The mountains serve as a kind of wallpaper, something you sometimes notice and say, "That's pretty." And he doubts if anyone at this party is noticing them much.

On the lawn are placed certain objects: a large table in the center containing food and drink, and at almost exact concentric intervals, white circular lawn tables, each circled with four matching chairs. This, then is the syntax: a dominant center, like a sun, some planets, each with four moons. The pattern is repeated in the circles of standing people making conversation—someone holding forth, the others listening and nodding. No one is sitting down.

Some parties are structured in straight lines. Those dreadful high school dances, for instance, with chairs all in a row. Other parties are—what?—equilateral triangles, maybe, with someone holding forth at the apex, the other people fixed into place at the base, supporting him. He's been to parties like that, where the host performs. But most parties fall into circles. One might see in this, he realizes, a proof of classical unity, with a kind of Ballanchine God choreographing all the successful parties of the world. But it breaks down under scrutiny, as all things break down.

It means nothing, for example, that Ian, that arrogant climber, is holding forth about his plans to live in Alaska. Without George and Susan there to gape at him, Ian wouldn't be at the center of anything. What they have, Peter thinks, is actually a triangle, in more ways than one, and so already the syntax of circles is breaking down.

Susan is tanned and arrogantly decorative in the way of women who muscle up in long flowing curves. She's a painter. Some say she's good, but her work is all about nature, and this is not too interesting. Her poor shmuck husband George keeps reaching for her hand, but she inches away. Peter thinks he'd like to walk over and take Susan's lovely muscular arm, see what that does to the syntax of her marriage. See what it does to his marriage.

Peter is a husband. He rolls the word inside his mouth like an unpalatable mouthful of food and feels the panic stir in his stomach as it always does when he remembers that he's married. It hasn't been all that long, and already the marriage has lost all meaning. He would like to spread wide his arms and flail at the air, for something beats at him, wants to crush.

He stands outside the circles and he feels incredibly alone. How could he ever explain this curious knotting up of terror and longing? He has waited a long time for someone to untangle him. He waits in silence like one of those sad-eyed nocturnal mammals for that delicate understanding, that passion of just the right intensity. Can't someone just bend over him and touch him with a cool and tender hand, really touch him?

Margaret has broken away from her little circle—where she is peripheral, as she always is, except to herself—and is flapping over to him like an anxious bird, beating her way among the others, not really seeing them. He wishes she were aloof and dark like Rita, a woman he couldn't fix into any pattern whatsoever. Even now, the thought of Rita stirs up a dull pain, and he thinks if he could have kept her in his life, he'd settle for meaning, illusory as it is.

22

Margaret's hair fluffs out like ostrich plumes as she moves toward him. The upper half of her body is ahead of the rest of herself. Everyone here will see how Margaret hovers over him, never letting him out of her sight, as transparent in her need for him as a child. She thinks she's the one to touch him. She's made a project of it, in fact. She will get through to her man. She will, by the sheer force of her sexual rapacity and her birdlike vigilance, crack him open.

He turns away from her approaching figure, moves toward the large table with the food and drinks. Automatically, he reaches down to take Robert's hand, except that Robert isn't here. He's home with a babysitter. He doesn't like leaving Robert with strangers. Margaret convinced him that the two of them ought to come to this party alone, and he is angry at this. The woman is jealous of a mere child. She speaks sincerely about being a parent to Robert because she needs to see herself as a good woman, but in truth there's nothing maternal in her at all. Out of the corner of his eye he sees Margaret watch him turn from her. There's puzzled hurt in her eyes, and she stops in her tracks, her arms drooping like broken wings. She stands there, and looks around herself as if she's lost. Peter wonders how much she will make him pay for that when it comes down to the hard bargaining of divorce. He shudders, not ready to think about that yet.

A year ago he did manage a trial run. He went so far as to take Robert off to California with him, letting Margaret think they weren't coming back. Then Lily did her suicide. He feels a little thrust of heat behind his eyes at the thought of Lily and the bravery of women who make strong and final choices. It would have looked bad if he hadn't come back then, and besides he had no intention of letting Margaret keep the house.

Drew is standing alone at the center table stabbing at vegetables with a toothpick. She's one of the few of Margaret's artsy nature-loving friends he respects, now that Lily's gone. Drew does good sculpture, plays with shapes in a way that tells him she knows about illusion and its losses. Margaret told him that Drew has just come back from a month in Wyoming at some artist's colony, which gives him something to say.

"How was Wyoming?"

She looks up at him as if she's surprised he'd know to ask. Like Susan, she is tanned, and her blunt-cut blonde hair falls across the side of her face like a brass blade. She pauses, then says, "I watched a lamb get born." She makes her voice tiny, almost lisping, as if she's mocking herself.

"Ah. That's something at least. You can't expect to take in all the sights." He picks up a black olive, pops it into his mouth.

She laughs, and he thinks that she's incredibly sexy, though he can't say just why. This reminds him of her husband, whom he also likes. "Where's Barry?"

She rolls her eyes to one side, shrugs. "He's gone. Didn't you know? He landed a big project in central Illinois. They're giving him a whole staff, the moon."

The loneliness comes back. He likes Barry very much, actually. He's the only person who knows more about computers than he does. Sometimes he'd get through a whole party talking to Barry about computers. But he recovers himself and remembers to ask, "Aren't you going too?"

She lays the flat of her hand against the blade of blonde hair, leans her face against it and looks up at him with her eyes, which seem to him as clear and open as a child's. "I love it here. The mountains, you know. But I suppose I will. He's my husband, after all."

Peter thinks he could talk her into staying here. He has a way with women and they generally do what he suggests. But this would imply responsibility for her, and he has already too much of that for Margaret and Robert. This is what's so terrible. Enjoy anything at all and before you know it there's some duty, some expectation. He could have most any woman he wants, this much he's learned, but any one of them would finally ask for the moon—except for Rita, who wanted nothing of him at all.

Drew is staring at him, as if she expects him to say something. He spears a slice of zucchini, hands it to her. "Yes, after all." He lets himself look sad. "We'll miss you." Then he moves over to the drinks, fills up a glass with ice. Drew leaves the table to join Ian and George and Susan, no doubt to talk about mountains. So much meaning people give to mountains! They're pretty, he'll admit, but so are women, some of them, and he'll be dammed if he'll wear himself out climbing all over them.

And he'll be dammed if he'll stand around any more. There are a lot of people he hasn't met yet, but these people are mostly Margaret's friends. He sits down in one of the moon-chairs, as far from the circles of conversation as he can get, and slips back into the shadows. What is different about an outdoor party? Do the people seem a little more self-conscious in the sunlight? The women swirl about as if they wore skirts and the men stand with their legs braced apart, hips thrust a little forward, thumbs hooked into belt loops. He narrows his eyes and zooms his mind back like a camera to take in the overall movement and sound of the party: It's a kind of waltz actually; a dipping and swaying, Tchaikovsky's flowers soaring and leaping, and then a pause, when no one speaks or moves, a nervous flutter, some tiny steps, and all at once swooping off again in some rhapsody of words. But he regains hold of himself. This is romantic drivel. Peter wishes he could take on the hard uncompromising edge of a true theorist, wishes the theorists (who would never come to this party) would accept him as one of their own.

He wants to put his head down on the round white table and weep. He doesn't think he's ever going to get to belong anywhere. The university doesn't value him. Robert will grow up and leave him; maybe when he's a little older he'll decide to live with Rita. Lily is dead and God knows what will become of his other graduates. Margaret is either rattling around in the kitchen being unhappy or off in the mountains. She's always trying to get him to come with her on those hikes, as if she thinks the experience will be so sublime he'll finally be hers. It's a shame. He loved her for a while. It might have worked. Maybe he'll apply for a job in California.

One of the circles explodes into laughter. He ought to be at the center creating that laughter. He has a gift for making people laugh, everyone tells him. But it's not a gift that comes easily in this unhappiness or with these people who don't think the way he does. He wants to be home with Robert, reading about pleasures of the text and watching baseball.

He feels suddenly, in fact, that he must go to Robert. It comes to him as a pang so sharp it makes him gasp. Something is wrong. Maybe he's hurt himself, gotten sick, a fire, or the babysitter. . . He rises and hurries to find Margaret.

She's on the edge of the laughing circle, not quite part of it. When she sees him coming toward her, her face breaks into a smile and she blushes like a young girl. This is what he can do to her, just by walking in her direction. It's a terrible responsibility. He takes her arm, pulls her away from the others.

"We've got to go home now," he says.

She frowns, and even then she's pretty. He'd wanted her because of all the women he knew, she was the prettiest, with hair fluffing out in separate strands as if she'd been tossed in the air by someone.

"Why?" she says.

"I'm worried about Robert." He wishes he didn't have to explain himself to her.

She is grimly silent for a moment, as if they've been through this before. "Well, why don't you call home and ask?"

"No." He is angry at the practical reasonableness of her suggestion. He doesn't want to come right out and say he's had a premonition and he knows that something terrible has happened to his son, so he draws himself up and says, "We're going. Now." Margaret always tells him he's good at sounding imperious, so why not?

She shrugs, tries too late to put a good face on it and smiles not very convincingly. They say a hurried good-bye to their host and hostess. Margaret is infected by his worry now. She remembers that the gas tank is on empty and says, "Do you think we'll make it home?" She plucks at the strands of her hair. He admits to her now that he just knows something has happened to Robert and starts up the car, gunning the engine. Then she has to run back to the party, where she's left her purse. By this time, both of them are nearly frantic.

The story line of fatherhood comes to him: you are laid out like a cable; someone plugs you in; you generate something, and you never get to roll yourself back up and belong just to yourself again. Tears rush into his eyes and he thinks he could not go on if something happened to his son.

They make it home on the empty gas tank and rush into the house. The babysitter looks up from where she's curled on the sofa, a little guiltily, for they've surprised her in the middle of eating some of their ice cream. "Where's Robert?" Peter cries.

The babysitter gets an odd look on her face. She points. There's Robert, on the floor where he always is, watching TV. He looks surprised to see them back so soon. Peter is struck, as he is every day, by how much his son looks like Rita.

Margaret is a study. Peter thinks it might be amusing to chart the flow of her thoughts, for she takes her role as a stepparent very seriously but she cannot reconcile this with her selfish desire for her man. What she probably cannot stand most of all is that she knows he wanted to leave the party anyway, but she can't accuse him of this because then she'd look like an uncaring parent. It's an interesting dilemma, and this pleases him. He is also dismayed, for he will pay for this somehow. Like a backwards meal, the syntax of marriage is this: dessert first, and then all the stuff that's hard to swallow, and then you go to the store, and you pay—and pay and pay.

Dear Lily

When Peter left me, I needed in the worst way that you should play a concerto for me. I needed something to move the tears out of me, to be with someone who would laugh and say, "Yes, Margaret, that's good." I didn't know you were already dead.

Remember our hike to the top of Lone Peak? Climb one of these mountains, you said, and you get to eat the world alive: the tang of fir and sagebrush, the salt of the big lake, the spun-sugar clouds spread wide by the sticky fingers of angels; take in, even, the groaning platter of the desert far to the south, and the underground rivers we know of only by faith and by the water we drink.

You told me that if I could get Peter to climb with me, he'd see. And he'd know that time is a thing you take into your arms like a lost child, give it food and blankets, give it love with all your injured heart. Being alive in time is not our last home, you said, and it can belong to anyone, like the land, and language, horses, birds, music. It's what I thought you believed.

The morning after I tried to reach you, Drew called to tell me you'd killed yourself. She said the landlord would let us into your apartment, and Susan was coming, too. We hurried to get there before your parents came and took everything away.

On every surface—the coffee table, the dresser, your piano—you'd created little shrines: a clump of dried lichen, a twist of juniper, a tiny bird's nest, some rocks, clustered here and there into miniature landscapes of desert, ocean, mountains.

What does this do to us, we who are trying to keep ourselves alive? Before this, we thought: for so long as we keep on making beauty, we will endure. You created beauty up until the very end, and it didn't save you.

Where does this leave us?

Why didn't you call me?

Why did you let me depend on you when it seemed that Peter might not love me any longer? You'd stroke my hair, smile into my eyes, promise trips together to the desert. Why did you take me up Lone Peak and say those things about time? Afterwards you cooked me dinner, complete with candlelight, homemade halevah, and French wine. Your thick dark hair fell across your perfect skin when you bent to blow out the candles. You smiled at me, your eyes a little sloed, making you seem exotic and uncommonly wise. "Margaret," you said. "Life is good."

There was that body you used to have, with which you sat a horse with natural grace, raced up a slope of scree, sliced through water like a sudden fish. I envied you that body; around you I felt ungainly and slow. You used to thrust out your legs to admire the new muscles, the wonderful skin in which each cell replaced itself softer and smoother than the one before. Your body was a home you lived in better than most.

Drew taught you how to ride horses, remember? Sometimes I came along to watch. There were hours of her calling out to you, "Heels down, eyes forward, give with your hands. Yes, that's nice, that's very nice." I see the astonished happiness in your upturned face, your body tipping forward and back in rhythm to the canter. When I brought Robert along, you helped lift him onto Drew's horse. You fastened his little hands to the pommel and walked beside to steady him as Drew led, told him how good he looked up there. And at Christmas, you brought him little gifts. Before Peter took him away to Los Angeles, Robert asked about you. I said I didn't know because I hadn't heard from you for a while. Now that he knows he is perplexed and sad. How does one explain unnatural endings to a child?

I'd known you for years before you'd play the piano for me. It took time, you said, to trust a friend enough for that. When you finally did, I wept because your music spilled out like a waterfall into a deep gorge, a cascade of sound that said all those things we keep hoping are true.

Like the stories you wrote, your music insisted against all the odds on one thing and one thing only: that we keep on feeling.

Your potted ferns foamed like fountains from the ceilings, splashed out onto the floor, and flowed into pools of sunlight. You must have loved your plants in a way that most of us never get to be loved.

You had two canaries, a mountain bike, a climbing rope, a small TV, an avalanche of books, a word processor, boxes filled with your stories, a refrigerator full of food. Drew and Susan and I wandered around, touching things, not speaking. We needed to absorb into ourselves what remained of you, quickly, before your parents, who did not seem to love you as we did, came and did whatever parents do with all the things belonging to their children that make no sense to them.

Grief, though it waited for us like a patient bird, seemed dangerous. Grief asks us to perform a kind of cannibalism: feast on the good memories, then sink our teeth into remorse for things not done, not said, and swallow, finally, the reality that with this person nothing will ever be done or said again. And then she is absorbed into our very cells; we learn to live with ourselves again, a little more than we were before.

How to do that with you? It would mean taking back into ourselves our own private terror of suicide, the lifelong temptation it is for some of us. Over the rim of your wineglass, you said, "We are women who cannot bear to be alone inside our bodies."

After we were done with roaming around your apartment, Drew and Susan and I huddled on the floor and tried to speak sensibly. How afraid we were! You had a right to your choice, we said. You had your reasons. We ought to respect that. Had there been warnings? Yes, we decided, though they were little more than brief allusions to death we'd taken as metaphors. And besides, how could we have stopped you? And then it got out of hand. We asked, what of those people who work day after day assembling toys that will break almost before they're used? What of the contractors who fling up houses on top of poisonous wastes, the lawyers who get rapists released on a technicality? How do all those people keep on living? We think we're immune to everyday despair because we write or sculpt or paint, appreciate music, climb mountains. But is what we do any better? How can any of us hope, we wondered, that our lives might matter, even a little bit?

And so on.

We had hoped we'd outgrown all this. You made it real again.

For me it seemed especially real. My own longing for death pulled at me like a summons. Peter had just moved to his sister's house in Los Angeles, saying he didn't think we could ever work things out. He took Robert, who is like my own child. And you weren't there to smooth back my hair, light the candles, let me cry, because you'd gone and done what I thought I would do if Peter left me. I was angry at you for abandoning me. And anger was a way of postponing the grief until it became less dangerous.

Drew and Susan and I left your apartment unable to look at each other or to perform the hugs and weepings that get people started on the feast of grief.

I telephoned Peter. This was something I'd promised myself not to do, but we are forced in extreme times to fall back on what we've known. He sounded shocked and saddened. You'd been his student, after all, one of his very best. He thanked me for telling him. I'd also promised myself I wouldn't beg, but his voice was my undoing: I told him I did not want to go through this life without him and Robert. Part of who you are lives inside the people you love. But people are such frail carriers! They go away. They die. You try to take yourself back or draw sustenance from what they gave you. But sometimes the process fails and your body gets lighter with that much less of you inside Contrary to what you once said, the books say that people can learn to live alone inside their bodies. If you've learned something about this now, please tell me.

We learned the details later the same day: a couple of deer hunters found you in your car on a back road up the canyon. You'd plugged the tailpipe, taped along the edges of the windows so there could be no mistake, curled up into a blanket like a small child. What do you suppose the hunters did once the police had come, taken their statements, taken you away? It is possible you saved the lives of a few deer that day. Perhaps those men went home and thought about everything in a new and grateful light. Or went out and got drunk, talked about leaving their wives.

Your parents. We could hardly bear to meet them. I can't call up a clear picture of what they were like, except that your mother chattered like a girl at a party, and your father kept saying, "If only she'd gotten married!" It must have been hard for them, must be harder now, impossible, with them alone together not even knowing what they ought to be missing. The funeral service did not seem to be about you. For one thing, the plants in the pale-carpeted parlor were made of plastic. Susan and Drew and I couldn't wait to get out of there, to feel the dry wind and the sagebrush tang rolling down from the foothills. As soon as the service was over, we huddled together in the parking lot and right then planned our own ceremony: to read your stories aloud and include you in our midst, to say good-bye. We would meet at my house in two weeks.

I thought, Girl, you've been enough of a fool, but I called Peter again and told him about the memorial we'd planned. And I said again, for there was nothing left to lose: I love you. Life is too short, I said, to spend on anger, on losses it is in our power to avoid.

Drew and Susan and I, with a few others from school, sat in a circle on the floor of my living room. We lit some candles. What did we accomplish at our little ceremony? What fiction did we invent to make coherent the story of your life and the reasons you took it? We decided on this: that you seemed to insist not only on feelings but on magic, a magic that enthralled your friends. Sometimes you acted as if singlehandedly you could create a perfect world. You'd planned, for one thing, to bring us together in a commune in the desert, where we could write and talk, go for hikes in the red-rock canyons and make gardens around an adobe house. We went along with your plans, unsure of how to pose our practical objections. And besides, what you gave us were our own dreams, our own hopes for community and closeness. And so I said things to you like, "Can we keep horses there? Let's do a cactus garden! Let's collect agates and make jewelry!" With how many grownups do you get to play like this? In this self-indulgence, I wonder, did I harm you?

You loved men who did not love you. We imagined that they, too, fell in with your delightful schemes and then betrayed them, left you as soon as your intensity became no longer a delight, but a burden. Your brilliance, your talent, your astonishing achievements seemed to count for little in your mind. You sometimes spoke with the voice of a bewildered child. Dark memories you had alluded to, things that should never happen to a child, but we weren't sure just what they were. You had reasons, we agreed, for what you did.

But, we said.

But take any one of us. We are like you, sort of. What then?

But never mind. We had begun by then to shore up our decision to stay alive. We lit some more candles and read aloud a chapter from one of your books, which was a story foretelling your own death, about a woman abandoned in the desert by the man she loves. You pulled it off with consummate skill.

Peter arrived just as the story ended. He hurried into the living room without taking off his coat, sat next to me on the floor, took my hand. Robert tumbled after, flung himself down into my arms.

I can't tell you any more about this, because it's too soon, too tenuous to be sure. Peter and I tear at each other's bodies like children at their Christmas gifts, like strangers in a bomb shelter. Any time now, we could find in each other what we're so hungry for—or it could all go up in fire and dust. Robert hovers around, smiling, anxious to please. Often, he rushes up to hug me. We get to celebrate you with the little bit we know of love, alive in whatever time we have left. Susan and Drew and I are shy around each other now, for a new uncertainty has come into our lives. We get hungry for the parts of you we couldn't take in. We miss you.

I haven't gone back up into the mountains yet, but I will sometime soon. I might even get Peter to come along and join me in that feast of time.

Sea Change

Then David told this story: "In Russia, certain women give birth in the sea. They squat naked in the shallows, supported by their husbands and midwives. There's almost no pain. Dolphins gather offshore, circle in close." David stroked his moustache, muffling his speech so the people in the room had to strain to hear him. "We come from the sea, all of us," he said. "The dolphins know this and they come to celebrate."

A little hush came into the room, and then Johann said in his loud voice, "New Age claptrap." Johann was head of Germanic languages and had known David and Sarah for a long time.

Sarah pressed her fist to her chest, leaned forward and said, "Oh no. It's been documented. There are pictures. We've seen them."

"There are pictures proving that the dolphins know we are all from the sea?" Johann settled back into his chair and smiled.

"I'm talking about the babies. These babies can swim within hours of birth. They're happy babies. Studies prove this. No colic, no colds. They're happy because the world was kind enough to receive them in their own element. That's what the scientists say."

"Wouldn't the blood attract sharks?" Johann's wife, Marlene, said.

Sarah felt shocked. David said, 'Not with all those dolphins around. Sharks are afraid of them, as anyone knows."

Marlene shivered. "It would be too cold. And what if people came to watch?"

David sat up tall. "In Russia, they don't worry about things like that."

"You and your Russia," Johann said. "It's a sick country. Why don't you accept this?"

And so there was nothing more to say. The four of them sat a while longer, so it wouldn't be obvious, but finally Marlene and Johann stood up to leave. After the polite good-byes and thank-yous, the Minkoff's gratefully shut the door behind the departing guests and turned as one to each other's arms.

"It was a mistake, telling them that story," David said.

"Oh no," Sarah said loyally. "It's a wonderful story."

"It was a mistake. I am not judging so well these days to whom I can say what." He led his wife to the bedroom, sat on the bed, and stared at the palm of his hand. "I think I'm losing my tolerance for wine."

"You're quite sober."

"But I am not quite right." He stared up at her. "How can I explain? I make these errors in judgement. I tell sacred things to the wrong people. I display myself."

Sarah sat down on the bed, kicked off her shoes. "You're being cruel to yourself because you were just with cruel people."

"They're not cruel. That's not the word. What is the word?"

"Small?"

"Well, yes. Perhaps that's it. They simply don't share our vision."

"Do you think we're being fair?"

"Perhaps not. I'm fond of them, I suppose, but I don't want to have them for dinner again. There aren't many people like us."

Sarah unpinned her hair, which she kept long because it made her feel still young, and thought that he sometimes held himself too high above other people, though holding themselves above other people was one of the things that had kept them together for so long.

He turned to Sarah, ran his fingertips down the side of her chin. The skin underneath had recently become crepy, and she closed her eyes against his noticing. He touched a strand of her hair. "You're always going to be lovely," he said. "Come, let's go to bed."

Sarah bent down, picked up her shoes, and placed them just so in the closet, as she always did. Their lives had settled into an order born of many years together in which they had quietly discussed their differences, agreed to work out even the smallest problem as it arose.

Everything had a place and was always returned to it. Every morning they arose promptly at six; David had the bathroom first because he was quickest; Sarah started the coffee, laid out the cereal and milk; while it was her turn in the bathroom, David fetched the newspaper, poured the coffee, laid out bowls and spoons. This routine was a great comfort to them both and freed them to live a life of the mind. They were, sensibly, atheists, having declared long ago that no higher being could preside over the sad, illogical world they found themselves in. Perhaps, they liked to think, they might improve this world a little bit with their scholarship and their appreciation of things beautifully performed and deeply felt. If the excitement had dimmed somewhat in recent years, then, no matter; they hadn't expected so very much. But sometimes a silence fell between them in sad little flickers, like snow, and they could not see what it was that connected them to each other.

Sarah woke up crying. In her dream she had been with David near the ocean, but they couldn't reach the shore. Every access was blocked by an odd assortment of barriers: ramshackle buildings, circus tents, cement walls, and mountains like the ones that loomed over the valley in which they lived.

Hearing her, David woke up and took her in his arms. He told her another story: "A woman went swimming in the sea with her baby. A dolphin swam up, cocked an eye at them, circled round and round as if to study them. After a while the dolphin swam away. Then it came back with a baby dolphin, as if to say, 'Now it's your turn to admire my child.'"

"That's beautiful," Sarah said, though the story made her want to weep some more. "Do you think if we'd been born under water, we'd be different?"

"How do we need to be different?"

"What if we'd had children?"

David fell away from her onto his pillow. "What if?" he said. "Why think about it? What would a child of ours do in a world like this?"

They had tried over the years to have children. Failing that, Sarah tried to grow a garden. The high desert soil in their Utah yard was sandy. She mixed manure into the soil, and, when that didn't help, humus, sphagnum moss, even chemical fertilizer. Finally the lettuce came up. She knelt over the seedlings and lost herself in the tiny swirls of leaves, the brave chartreuse of newborn green. The next morning the leaves were all gone, eaten by the snails. She bought snail-killer pellets. But the sight of dead snails and poisonous pellets everywhere made her feel ill, and she abandoned the garden.

They spent their evenings reading or grading papers and exams. They taught languages at a small university in northern Utah. He taught Russian. She taught it when there was demand for another section, which was not often, but she also taught French. They knew they were lucky to have jobs at the same university. And they knew that if a language weren't required for an Arts degree, they'd have no jobs at all, for not many students chose to major in foreign languages these days.

"University students are declining in quality," David said, as he often said. "Hardly any of them study Russian anymore. How can a person be educated, not having read Tolstoy in the original?"

Sarah didn't reply, for it wasn't necessary, but she set down the book she was reading and looked at her thoughts for a while. Then she said, "Tell me, dear, just what is our vision?"

"Pardon me?"

"Our vision. You said the other night that Johann and Marlene don't share our vision, and I've been wondering just what our vision is."

David looked hurt. "How can you ask such a thing? It isn't the sort of thing you can answer point-blank. It's something you understand or you don't."

"Of course I understand, but if I try to think about it, the phrase flits away like a fish. Our vision. I ask myself, what does 'our vision' mean?"

"Take anything and say it long enough, it has no meaning at all"

"But it's important and I've lost it. Nothing seems quite certain any longer."

David sighed, stretched out his hand and gazed at his palm, traced the lines in it with his fingertip. "It's all too certain, my Sarah. We live in a country that doesn't care about beautiful things."

"That's a criticism, not a vision."

"We see what we can. We're lost in a lost world."

Next to the abandoned garden was a pear tree. Every summer Sarah harvested these pears and was shocked anew that they were tasteless, hard, inedible. She walked outside into the twilight, leaving David in his armchair. She stared at the meager white spring blossoms on the pear tree, then picked off a branch, saying, "You might as well be good for something," carried it into the house, set the sparse spray of blossoms in a vase and placed it on the mantel.

"We have to get out of here," she said to David. "Now that we aren't seeing Johann and Marlene, we don't have any friends to share our hearts and souls with. The garden is impossible; even the pear tree won't give us anything." She swept her arm toward the branch, which looked Oriental and austere against the white wall.

David was gazing at his hand, first the back of his hand, then his palm, turning it slowly, cocking his head from side to side. He had taken to doing this lately, sometimes by the hour. He had very beautiful hands, with long slender fingers, but Sarah didn't think that was the reason why he was doing this. He looked up at her, his eyes watery and unfocused, and said, "The pear tree?"

The next night, he called to her to come to him. She stood before him in front of his chair. "I need you to tell me something, Sarah."

"I'll try."

He held out the back of his hand to her. "Touch me."

She brushed the dark hairs on his hand with her fingertips.

"Harder."

She pressed her fingers down on the strong veins, careful not to slide the slackening skin and reveal that he, too, was getting old in the hands, where people seem to show their age no matter what the rest of them is like.

"Tell me," he said, "Am I really here?"

She wanted to laugh, but her respect for him restrained her. "Of course you're here."

"I'm not sure these days. Something's wrong with me. I keep making terrible mistakes." He looked up at her with stricken eyes. "In class today, I told them I believe in God."

She decided then, took action. She presented him with the tickets the very next night, saying, "The day finals are graded, we're leaving. We're going to the ocean. We're going to stay for the summer. No arguing." She could, when necessary, be strong with him. When he didn't say anything, she said, "We've never been to the ocean in all our twenty years!"

He sat there, passive as a child. "I'm remembering things," he said. "I remember my mother's face. Isn't that odd?"

He can't possibly remember her face, she thought. The woman had died when he was a baby, and all the pictures had burned with the house. He'd been taken by an aunt from Russia to America soon after. He wasn't even really Russian, nor was she, having been born in New York. It was time for them to take hold.

She'd chosen Oregon, because the travel agent had said there weren't many tourists and there were open beaches where you could walk the entire coast if you had a mind to. They flew to Portland. Sarah rented a car and drove them down to Lincoln City. They arrived at their oceanfront cottage after midnight, smelling and hearing the surf but too tired to say anything about it. They slept so soundly it was as if they'd sunk into the deepest part of themselves, and to wake up was a struggle upward, requiring enormous effort. They opened their eyes, sat up, stared at each other, slow and careful, like divers wary of the bends. It was nearly noon.

When they picked their clothes up off the floor where they'd dropped them the night before, they staggered a little, as if stunned by a blow. Sarah brushed her hair, but didn't bother to pin it up into a twist as she usually did. Neither of them opened the curtains to look out the window, which they knew would reveal an excellent overlook of the ocean. They walked slowly to the main street of the town, ate breakfast at the first cafe they saw, and lingered over many refills of coffee. At home they always limited their coffee to two cups a day.

Sarah shook herself, blinked, and said, "Why are we so slow today?"

He rubbed an eye with the heel of his hand. "Slow?"

"This isn't like us. It frightens me a little."

He took her hand, smiled. "What is like us? We are what we are being, that's all."

"What I think is that we're scared to go."

"Go where?"

"To the beach. Where else would we be going?"

He leaned back, looked very tired. "Yes, I think you're right. There isn't anyplace else for us to go."

"That wasn't my point."

He stood up suddenly. "I'm going to find a paper." When he returned, he sat down heavily across from her and said. "I've always wanted to tell you this: your points are never very clear." Then he slipped off the first section of the newspaper, shook the crease out of it, and began to read.

She caught hold of the edge of the paper and said, "You're being cruel. I don't understand."

He frowned at her. "Are you sure you don't mean 'small'?"

She shook her head. "No. Yes. Both."

He stroked his moustache with the curl of his finger. His eyes looked distant and bored. "This trip was your idea," he said. "I would have preferred a vacation in the mountains, which we live next to, never appreciate."

"Why didn't you tell me?"

"I Just realized it myself. Besides, it wouldn't have done any good, telling you."

She stood up and said, "That story about the dolphin bringing her baby. That *is* New Age folklore. It's just a made-up story, means nothing."

He blinked, seemed to recover himself, picked up the newspaper and lowered his eyes to read. She reached for her purse and said, "I'm going to go now. I am going to the beach. I don't understand this at all." She hurried out of the restaurant, her eyes blurry with tears. Never, since those first few difficult years, had they hurt each other like this. Her husband had stared at her as if she were a faintly distasteful stranger.

But she could not bring herself to go to the beach alone. It was something the two of them must do together. She regretted her flight from the cafe, decided she'd been too sensitive, too easily hurt. And so she would wait for him in the cottage. Then they would go to the beach together—or wait another day, if that's what he needed. She lay on their unmade bed and listened to the waves, which had a double thump to them, she noticed, like enormous heartbeats, perhaps like the heartbeats of great sleeping whales—if whales ever slept, and surely they did. Probably they even dreamed. And perhaps they cried in some way of their own when the dreams were sad, which surely they were.

When she awakened, it was nearly sunset. She leaped up, alarmed, confused, unsure of where she was, bewildered about the time. And where was David? It was cold in the cottage and she longed for them to be back their house in Utah just as they'd always been. She threw on a sweater and hurried out the door, then stopped, unsure of where she ought to go. He couldn't possibly still be in the cafe, but perhaps, like her, he'd decided to wait.

The cafe was closed. The dimness inside was like the eye of a large animal, telling her nothing. The police? Night after night he'd stared at his hands. And then he'd told his class that he believed in God, told her he'd seen the face of his mother. Thinking of this, she suddenly saw him as alien and strange, the way she had once seen her father when he'd drunk too much and become a person from a country she didn't know.

Then she felt ashamed. Perhaps David was ill and she hadn't been loving enough to see and to help him. Or perhaps, away from the graceful not-seeing of everyday routine, he had glimpsed a flaw in her for the first time, realizing suddenly how she was aging and would never give him a child or how sometimes her mind was not always clear. But no. He was a kind man. He would never just leave her like that. No. Something was very wrong for him, pressing him down, pulling him under.

She hurried off the main street of the little town, down the narrow network of roads leading to the shore. She looked into the cottage in case he'd come there in the meantime. He wasn't there. She hurried down the narrow street running parallel to the shore. The path to the beach cut steeply down a sandbank fringed with swatches of beach grass. The beach was enormous, a wide pale expanse that curved along miles of coastline in both directions. The ocean seemed very far away.

She stepped around the driftwood piled up against the bank, then tried to hurry through the heavy sand, sinking into it like a desperate dreamer. When she finally reached the glittering stretch of hard damp sand, she broke free into a run. The air smelled of seaweed and dead fish. Flocks of little silver birds ran across the sand like sudden masses of light. The surf, calm as a lake, lapped around spires of black rock exposed by the low tide. The sun had slipped behind the haze of the ocean horizon and came through muted and soft in the colors of Easter.

The light wouldn't last much longer, and so she ran to the fluted edge of the sea, cast her eyes among the rocks that stood in the shallows like a crowd of waders, called his name and despaired of finding him.

Russia! He's gone home! He's gone to find his mother. She sat on the edge of the surf and put her face in her hands. Gulls mewed like babies and the foamy tips of the sea began to touch her feet, but she could not move.

She felt a hand on her head. Then he was lifting her to her feet and then his arm was tight around her. He was carrying his shoes and his pants were rolled up to his knees. In the fading light, she could barely make out his face.

"Thank God," he said.

"Yes," she said, "Thank God."

"I've looked for you here for hours. I just now thought to look in the cottage. You weren't there. I've been terribly worried."

She bent her head, ashamed now of her terrible worry for him.

He pressed a smooth stone into her hand. "I found this for you."

"Oh?"

"It's an agate. You can hold it up to a lamp and see the light come through it. That's how you know."

She stepped away, turning her shoulder to him as if to say, "I need more than a stone."

"It's beautiful here. But I couldn't find you. I was so sorry for the way I spoke to you. And then I thought . . . never mind." He pressed his hand into her waist, said, "It's cold. Let's go home." They trudged through the heavy sand, leaning on each other as though they'd been rescued from something. On the path threading up the sandbank, he said, "Before I left the cafe, I called Johann and Marlene."

"Whatever for?"

"I invited them to stay with us for a week."

"Are you crazy?"

"Yes."

"That's all you're going to say—yes?"

She felt him shrug, pulled away from him, and said, "I hate it here."

"I hate it here, too. But that isn't what you meant to say. What you meant to say was, you hate to see anything change for us, even for the better."

She had nothing to say to that.

"I'm not really crazy, you know. In fact, you were right."

"About what?"

"We haven't been fair. Johann and Marlene are good friends. So what if they're different about some things? They're like us in the important ways."

"So long as we don't talk about Russia."

"You were right about another thing."

"Oh?"

"About being afraid. I have wanted this for so long, I was afraid it wouldn't be wonderful enough. And now that I know better, I'm afraid I am going to start believing in things I don't believe in."

He laughed. "That's what I meant when I said I hate it here, which I didn't mean any more than you did, though I do think we need to start going up into the mountains when we get home. Being here makes me afraid of what I might find out about myself. And perhaps my reasons for being here have something to do with wanting to find—do I dare to say this—God. Does that make you afraid?"

"Yes." But the fear was like the cool ocean wind. The shivering made her feel, perhaps, alive.

Strands of her hair lay tangled and salty across his bare shoulder. The sheet beneath her was damp. Through the open curtains, the sun fell across the bed like a fresh idea. She lay still, wanting to prolong this moment of waking up. He slept in a new way, his arm flung over his head, palm upward, his head tilted back like a man welcoming rain. It was as if he had finally abandoned himself to whatever might come to him in the night. What, exactly, did come to him then? Or did he go somewhere else, a place far away from her? She felt a pang of jealousy, thinking this. But then there were her dreams, which, although she told him about them, could never be told exactly as she'd felt them. She wished she could escape this circling back to being alone, never fully at one with something or someone else.

He stirred and opened his eyes, blinked at seeing her staring at him. He turned on his side and took a fistful of her hair as if it was a swatch of grass he might uproot, released her, and said, "I had this incredible dream. I dreamt that everyone in the world was caught in an enormous tidal wave and we were swimming in such a way that we bumped into each other and changed into the person we bumped into. No one minded. It was a kind of game, everyone laughing and bumping and changing faces and bobbing up and down. It gave me the most wonderful feeling. Why, do you suppose?"

"It sounds scary to me," Sarah said. "I wouldn't want to change like that."

He sat up and smiled down at her. "No one would, probably, but maybe it would be a good thing. No more identity crises, just imagine!" He leaped out of bed, reached his hand to her. "Come, let's go for a swim."

"They say the water's too cold for swimming here," she said.

"Russians don't worry about such things," he said.

He splashed into the surf, which was just beginning to ebb, pulled her after him. The shock of the water made her gasp, and to keep moving was the only way she knew she had a body left at all. He stopped, smiled, and slipped off his swimming trunks. She looked back at the empty beach, then wriggled out of her swimsuit. David took it from her and ran to a log on the shore, flung the swimwear over it, ran back to Sarah where she shivered in the surf. When they'd gone out far enough, they swam together, diving, rubbing legs against legs, hands reaching for an ankle, a breast, all the parts of themselves, which at home had become, if not tedious, then too known to surprise them. It was a weaving dance they did in the water, bringing them together and apart and together again, all the weight gone from them.

"Open your eyes," David shouted as they bobbed to the surface.

She coughed, shouted back, "They are open."

"I mean underwater. We need to watch for the rocks."

And so they dived under again and opened their eyes. Ripples of sand and dark peripheral masses of ragged rock burned into their vision. Her long, loose hair undulated between them, alien and green like a strange kind of seaweed. Their numbing hands fluttered before them in the currents like slow-moving birds. They no longer knew which part of themselves they kept as their own, which part belonged to the sea.

Cold Hands

It's early October, and the valley where we live glows warm and red in the tender fist of Indian summer. But up here in the Wasatch Mountains something has let go, like dice flung from a reckless hand. The air suspends our breath in sudden disbelief. A fog of swirling ice particles shuts out the sun. The rocks are glazed with ice. An easy scramble up to the peak and across the ridge to the Snowbird tram has become a challenge, and we aren't prepared. George, my husband, has forgotten his gloves. Ian, our leader, has brought only one rope for the six of us. Of course, we decide to go ahead. I laugh nervously, and Ian says, "Susan, didn't I tell you? Any climb with me is going to be an epic."

George and I have climbed with Ian before. There was that spire of granite at the City of Rocks, an apparent easy few pitches that took us hours to climb because every crack petered out in the middle of nowhere, the crystals were rotten, and the friction pitches were slick with lichen. I was so tired on the rappel down I nearly let go of the rope.

And here I am, about to embark on yet another epic climb, this time not just with Ian and George. Ian has invited three young climbers to come along. He likes to include everyone he meets in his adventures. I would never say this to George, but I think I'd follow Ian anywhere, even though he frightens me. Maybe it's because nothing bothers him and I'd like to learn to be that way. I'm a person, my mother always said, who's bothered all too easily, and I want to be a bigger person than that. I want to be as large as the sweep of a cirque, as inexhaustible as the rocks that break away and still loom thick and

46

implacable as God. But as I tie into the rope for the first pitch up the ice-coated rock, what I am is a small-minded knot of fear.

Ian belays us up each pitch one at a time, which requires much tedious tying and untying and a long wait every fifty feet or so. Each step up, each handhold, has to be exactly right, for the ice is dead smooth and filmed with melt-water. Sometimes the sun comes through, a pale disk in the ice-fog, faceless as a washed-out moon. Time is not something we think about. What we measure is the angle of our bodies against the rock, the intake of breath as we commit our weight to another toehold, another curl of fingertips around the slippery edge of a crack.

Ian reaches the peak first. The sun explodes out of the fog, and the ice-coated rocks become a tumbled dazzle of gold. His black hair is wild and electric against the backlight of the naked sun. He helps us over the top one at a time, reaching out his bare hand, which is warm and very strong. The six of us stand silently, the fog and the sudden blazes of light swirling around us like uncanny music. Then the three young climbers raise up their arms and cavort on the peak as if they've won something. They shout and yodel; like me, they can no longer stand so much beauty, but have to celebrate and shatter the spell in the same instant.

Sometimes when the moon washes through our window like an old river I feel George's hands scooping into where my soul lives as if to sift out the gold, and I think it's the beginning of what they call joy. I think I'm finally going to be known, and being known is, after all, what we were born longing for. But then a shadow crosses the bed like a raptor and it feels like I'll be carried off and torn and eaten, so I push his hands away and think of something else—colors, maybe, and shapes, and the pressure of granite against the sky, a painting I want to begin—or I think of Ian, because he would never undo me with love that way; he'd make me strong. He'd hold me at arm's length and say, "Susan," and not think I was all mixed up in who he is.

The fog closes in again and we stand on the summit silent now, and afraid, though no one actually says this. It took us five hours to reach where we are. We still have a long razorback ridge to cross before we reach the tram, and it will be dark in a few hours. And so Ian says we have to make what climbers call a suicide line—all of us tied into the same rope about ten feet apart.

"But," I say, "if one of us falls, we all fall."

"Susan," he says, "I'll catch you. I promise," and his mountain-wise eyes stare into mine with the light of all those promises you've always hoped someone would make.

A razorback ridge is a few feet wide at best, laid out with tilted slabs of pointed rock, loose boulders and bearing-like stones. Each side, we know, drops away sharply for hundreds of feet, though the fog keeps us from seeing just how exposed we are. We take a long time getting ourselves organized on the rope. George fumbles with the knots and says, "My hands are cold."

Except for Ian, George is the toughest climber in the group, and for him to say that means his hands are very cold indeed. I feel a sudden and terrible sadness for him. I ought to hurry across the icy stones, unzip my jacket, take his hands, and say, "Armpits. Keep them there a while." He'd slip his hands into my jacket, smile, and squeeze at my breasts. He'd be grateful and reassured. What's wrong with me that I can't give him this? What kind of wife doesn't want the hands of her man inside her coat?

As long as the fog stays thick, we move across the ridge disembodied and flat, unaware of the beauty and the risk. But a squarish patch of fog tears away and we're given a perfectly framed glimpse of Mount Timpanogas, the Sleeping Lady, laid out some twenty miles away, a tragic figure in tatters of snow. Aspen are scattered at her base like offerings of gold. And below us, the fog crumbles away like a failed foundation, and we can see the dark plunge of scree and, below that, a sheer fall of granite.

We are strung out on the rope across the ice-coated ridge like beads on a rosary. A hand from the sky could come down and pray on us: grace and fruit and bread. My mother could rise up and walk beside me and say, at last, "I'm with you." My father, who was a far cry from Our Father, could climb over the dark edge and say, "I'm proud of you, even if you're only a daughter."

George, who is the bead behind me, keeps saying that his hands are cold, and this makes me angry now, for I think, "What sort of man can think of his hands in the face of The Lady and the people we've lost and the nearness of death?

It is possible that I'm a bigger person than my parents thought I was—but how could they have thought much at all, so taken up with dying? When George came into my life I thought I was small as a vole, a scurrying undergraduate, afraid I had no gift to lay at the feet of the world. George swept his hand across my hair, traced the lines of my face with his finger, helped me to believe. He loves me so intently, his golden eyes so frozen into me, I think he wishes I would stop breathing. I think he wishes I weren't getting to be a pretty good climber, weren't now a graduate student or what they call a rising talent. He tugs on the rope behind me, as if to say hello, and I feel that he's trying to shrink this moment, these mountains, into something he can manage.

And maybe he does. The fog covers the Sleeping Lady, lays out its blind floor once again, and we trudge in the stolid comfort of zero visibility, nothing to deal with except the next step, the place where a hand needs to grab across a jagged slab. The world is the size of my boot, the measure of purchase on a patch of black ice or a nubbin of granite, nothing ahead except a rope receding into dim whiteness. This is enough; this is all there truly is. Whatever was it I thought I should have?

Then the fog opens a new window to a glistening ice-tipped fir awash in a shatter of prism like spray in a sunlit whitecap. It is impossible not to stop and gasp and take in that color and light and to be once again disturbed and restless and wanting. Mountains astonish you and make you reach. You think the whole world is generous like this, with room for all the longings, the terrible excesses. I can feel this reaching in the line, a tension that keeps us apart, keeps us together, makes it difficult to remember where we're going. And then to our left, the fog tears away to an impossible purple of mountains layered in the great distance like folds of a velvet robe. It's like being in an enormous art gallery where the paintings flash onto a white wall, disappear, flash somewhere else, then somewhere else again. I'm a landscape artist, and I would not be foolish enough to try to make real a glory like this. How can anyone seeing this not think that everything is possible?

George loses his footing. I feel the sudden lurch of it and turn to see him kneeling on a slab of shining rock, his hands rubbing each other in a kind of supplication. "My God!" I yell, "we'll all be killed!" I'm afraid we won't reach the last tram, and I don't think I could endure the long climb down in the darkness. I'm afraid of falling and I'm angry beyond reason, wishing not to be tied into that rope, my life so inextricably bound up, held down, kept in line, with his.

And there is this, I see too suddenly, too soon: I want to lie down in the promises in Ian's eyes. Why? Is it because he's the leader and we all desire leaders? Is it because his hand was warm when he reached down for me at the peak? Yes, and yes, but no, I think it is because I want not to be bound to anyone and I want to experience everything in this stunning and dangerous world.

There is no one to tell this to. Is *telling* something a person ought to be able to do without? I think that many people live with no one to tell things to. I am surely not the only one who miscalculates, who wants everything, risks too much.

I had, for example, a friend, Lily, who could do everything. She could play classical piano and write achingly beautiful stories and ride horses and survive alone in the desert. She killed herself not long ago. None of us quite knows why, but I think it was because it hurts too much to have nearly everything when you know that the one little thing you need the most, which is love, small as a footprint, is never going to happen.

Some people might think it's a hard thing to climb an ice-covered mountain. I will admit I'm afraid up here; I'm cold; I'm tired. But there are ways to fix the mind so you can do it. To love takes far more courage. When you love, your mind runs away from you, leaves you with feelings impossible to manage. I think love isn't something I'm going to get to learn how to do, not in a way that can last. Maybe I'll go after Ian's love, which means I'll try once again to wrest love out of myself, and when that finally fails, I will do the only honest thing for a person like me, which is to be alone. My mother used to say, "Susan, a person as bothered as you will always be alone." I want her to be wrong in this, but it is, as they used to say, written.

In the meantime, none of us on this mountain is alone. In a few hours we'll untie ourselves and walk to our separate cars, go down into the Indian summer valley. But here and now, we get to love. A great happiness rises in my chest like an early moon. Perhaps this is everything, but I won't be able to hold onto this, not even as an idea. Maybe love isn't a feeling that lasts, but if it's acted upon, it gets to be real for a little while.

George acts; he does everything for me: he's building me a studio, putting me through school; he brings me tea in the morning. But sometimes when he goes at a granite face on a climb or hammers in a new wall in the studio, I see a rage beneath that ever-giving love. I see a man who in his giving would smother me in downy feathers and keep me afraid and confused by his goodness. This is a love I must soon escape. I can't say if this is because his rage is a real thing I rightly fear, or if I'm inventing it because I am one of those women who can't accept a good man. Either way, I think I'm going to have to leave George, and this makes me inexpressibly sad. I want to do something for him, show him what little bit of love I've found on this mountain.

I tug on the line ahead of me to stop the climbers in front and call for some slack. The rope relaxes like an exhaled breath. Then I pick my way back across the ridge to where George is kneeling and rubbing his hands. I crouch beside him, take his hands in mine, huff my warm breath onto his white fingers. He raises his face to mine and his eyes are like wet aspen leaves. I pull off my gloves and hand them to him. He shakes his head. "It's only a little longer," I say. "My hands will be fine."

He nods, rises to his feet, and takes the gloves, tries to pull them on, but they catch at the knuckles. "They're too small," he says.

"Curl your fingers inside the bottom part," I say.

"Then I won't be able to hold the rope," he says.

"You don't need to," I say. "Remember? You're tied in."

"Yes. Of course." He shakes his head as if he's just awakened in a strange bed. "Thanks."

We reach the last tram in darkness, tumble into it, breathless and ruddy, tied into one another. We are laughing. The three young men leap and yodel. Our noses drip from the cold and we wipe them on our sleeves. Ian begins to supervise the untying and the gathering up of rope, but his eyes are already beginning to move away from us to the next mountain. George and I hug one another and cry out, because right now there's love, and why not take it? "We made it!" we shout. How wonderful, how brave we were!

The Importance of Birds

"Robert and I had a close call." Margaret is still shaken, and the words are interrupted by little gasps. "We were sitting on this big rock near the waterfall up the canyon near Snowbird. A huge avalanche came down the waterfall and buried the rock. I knew enough to run, so we escaped with our lives." She's proud that she isn't using too many words, for she usually goes on about a thing too much. Robert leans against her, his shoulder pressed to her hip. His hair, which she cuts herself, is damp across his forehead.

Peter hooks his arm around her waist, something he hasn't done for a while, and says, "You saved my son's life." Then he releases her, bends to Robert, picks him up and carries him to the sofa, which is their place for being together.

She perches herself on the arm of the sofa. "Wasn't there an old Chinese custom about saving a life?" she asks him. But no, he hasn't heard of such a thing. And does it matter?

Something in Margaret is restored by this narrow brush with death. She sleeps the whole night through and wakes up early in the morning in the old forgotten way, alert and filled with the sense of possibility. She turns in the bed and presses herself to her husband, no longer minding the prickle of the hairs on his back. And she does not hold her breath and hope that he will relax his body against hers. She won't be needing to do that now.

She eases herself away from him and goes to the window, which overlooks the valley and the range of mountains to the east. Although it's late spring, the mountains are capped with snow. These snowy mountains are no longer merely beautiful, but are forces in their own right, for they almost enfolded her and Robert in whiteness like angels.

She dresses quickly, bending stiff-legged to tie her shoes for the sheer pleasure of stretching the backs of her legs. She likes to use her body and likes that it be used. A hard fall on a ski slope, knuckles scraped in a climb. Good. The body's getting used. The body is here, alive, feeling what it feels, even when it hurts, and even more so when it soaks in a warm bath or feels the man inside. She used to leap onto Peter and tussle with him, wanting the push and pull of him, the power of his arms, her arms, his force against her own. "Let's wrestle," she'd say. And he'd say, "No." And then, "Why not?" A silence, and then he'd tell her: "I'd win." No matter how she tried to explain, he couldn't see that winning was not the point at all. Even though Peter had come back to her from California after he'd said he wasn't going to, she didn't feel the least bit happy when he'd said, "You win."

Robert is always up before her, no matter how early. The child, she knows, has trouble sleeping. He sits in the dark windowless living room with the TV turned up much too loud. Before the avalanche, it made her angry to see him cross-legged on the floor awash in the watery electronic light, his little mouth gaping open like a guppy's. Now, as she descends the stairs, she realizes how unimportant her anger was, and how dear he is, no matter what.

For—and this comes to her suddenly—she is now his mother. Before this, being a mother was a set of rules in her mind: act this way, do this, refrain from that—tell him to brush his teeth, be nice to him, be fair. If you get angry, try not to yell. This was a not a bond, but a caste system: "I'm the grownup, I get to tell you what to do; you get to be a kid—within certain limits." Sometimes this felt like love, but then she wondered if that was just because loving was one of the rules for being Mother.

Now, Mother is a feeling as heedless and inevitable as the great plumes of snow curling like waves over the mountain cornices. These plumes settle like feathers. So many feathers! Piling on and piling on, melting and freezing until they change into ice pellets and bond in a mass that cleaves to the concave cirque like a Great White Father.

When the tension builds, the mass of snow swells outward like a belly, ripe for a great and terrible birth.

Saving a life, birthing a life are perhaps nearly the same thing, and then you're responsible forever. This is the Chinese custom Peter said he didn't know: if you save a person's life, you're committed to that person's welfare for as long as he then lives. This seems to explain why she should suddenly know she loves the child, but it does not explain why this discovery should carry with it such astonishing pain.

The boy comes to her in the kitchen as she waits for the kettle to boil, hugs her, long and tight. Yes. He looks up at her with his gap-toothed smile and says, "I love you." Then he pours himself some milk, goes back to the TV. She drinks her coffee in the kitchen, deciding wisely to stay out of the living room, where she would be forced, for her own sanity, to turn down the volume. No longer will she impose her wishes on these two males who have let her into their lives. How lucky she is!

Peter comes downstairs. She rises to greet him, filled with the joy and sorrow of her new understanding. She wants him to sweep her into a long close hug, but he doesn't like long hugs, and from now on she's going to respect what he doesn't like. Too much, too often, she has asked for this and for that: touch me here; hold me a little longer; talk to me; please don't turn away from me; please can I turn down the TV. Too much. Life can end in an instant of sudden whiteness. You take what you have, this moment, and that's enough.

She turns to the sink and rinses out a sponge, thinking she'll clean the inside of the refrigerator. A different kind of bird has come to the feeder by the window above the sink. Finches of some sort, a lovely desert red and yellow. The females, of course, are plain, but in their coloring, traces of sage and sandstone. It bothers her that she can't name them.

She couldn't have been more than a few years older than Robert is now when her Aunt Mary taught her the names of birds. She spent a whole summer with Mary while her parents went off somewhere, she doesn't remember why. Mary was happy to have her, for her own children had been taken away from her by divorce decree and she'd never seen them again. Mary was president of the local Audubon

Society. Her house was filled with Audubon prints, little porcelain birds, pieces of speckled eggshell, empty nests.

Margaret will have to look up the finches in the guide. She thinks of calling Robert into the kitchen to see the birds, but they'll come back. Not every moment has to be seized. There's time. There's time. She wonders why she must remind herself of this. Time, of late, has seemed to be something she's running out of. Now she breathes in deeply and thrusts her hands under the warm tapwater, feels that she has a future again.

"I'm going to the office," Peter says. He never goes to the office in the morning. She was hoping that after Robert left for school they'd spend some time together, maybe make love. She won't ask for this. There's a great deal for her to learn not to ask. She notices the hurried look in his eyes and reaches into the open door of the freezer, needing the icy air against some other thing hot and fisted up.

After Peter leaves, she calls Robert to her, points to the birds outside the window. He presses up against her, rises on tiptoe and says, "Oh wow!" but he's being polite and it's time for him to get ready for school. She wonders if his mother has disappeared for good this time, or if soon the poor woman will return to reclaim her son. The trick is not to want anything too much. How, if you have become responsible, do you accomplish this?

The next morning, instead of getting up, she turns away from Peter and goes back to sleep, another new thing. She falls into the strange dreams that seem to come only in late-morning slumber. She dreams about an avalanche. The snow is a great wall stretching for miles, and moves toward their house. She's running back and forth between her husband and Robert, shouting, "Run! Danger!" But they don't seem to hear her.

She wakes up slowly, feeling great loss and dread, takes her time going downstairs. Robert has gone to school. Her husband is lying on the sofa reading. She sits next to him. "The avalanche was really loud," she says. "Like a train." He smiles up at her. "It was a very close thing, for both of us."

As she says this, she is seized with a sudden anger that not once has he shown concern that she, too, was nearly killed. And so it is not enough just then that he squeezes her hand, and that he takes up his book again so quickly is an affront. The news channel is on and it's too loud. With great effort of will, she speaks of none of these things.

At dinner, which they customarily eat in front of the TV, she waits for a commercial and says, "They say spring avalanches are the worst, because the snow is so heavy it sets up like cement."

Her husband looks up at her politely, his forkful of food poised in midair.

"There must have been a huge snowfield high above the waterfall. You couldn't see it from where we were, so when I first felt the big drops of water I couldn't figure out what was happening."

Peter returns his fork to his plate, nods to her, picks up the remote control, switches through the channels.

Robert looks up at them from the floor, where he sits cross-legged to eat. "Margaret saved my life," he says.

"Come here," his father croons. He pushes aside his plate and holds out his arms. He and Robert lie together on the sofa until Robert's bedtime. What a loving father! But she feels unhappy. Since their return from California, Robert often leans himself against her, as if he'd like to lead her into the circle of touching. But Peter seems to shut her out and she does not know why.

She wakes up at four in the morning and thinks of a possible reason: Peter is afraid he won't get to keep Robert. The last time Rita took Robert for the day, he'd said, "What if she tries to get custody now?" But Rita hasn't called or written for almost a year. Margaret, he knows he can keep. She can't hide how much she loves him, and so, he shouldn't worry about losing her. A person has to know there's someone who will stick with you, no matter what.

She rubs her hand over the little hairs on his back, then touches his up-arched hip. She would like to take hold of this hip and rock him, get him unstuck. He feels like a mired boulder. She wants him to roll, wants to tumble after. It is all she can do to keep herself from going at him. He hitches himself away from her hand and sighs, as if something sad has come into his dreams.

She falls asleep again and sleeps once again late into the morning. This time the avalanche is black, closer to the house, taller. She can see the layers of crust, the granules where the strange dark snow had melted, frozen up again. She tries to get Peter to look out the window to see for himself, but he won't. She's wild with fear, weeping and wringing her hands. This fear stays with her even after she wakes up. She takes a long time getting dressed and is nervous about going downstairs to face her two men. Something needs to be done, but she doesn't know what it is.

Her husband takes her to their Chinese dinner on Saturday night. It's a custom she's held him to, because it's the one time they get to sit across from each other at a table. But she's uneasy, knowing he resents the obligation. She wishes she could release him from his sense of duty, free him into something light and easy, like having fun. But she thinks his idea of fun would not include her. And she has finally learned not to ask head on: "What's wrong? Why won't you look at me?" She tries to say entertaining things, coaxes him to talk about his problems at the university, a subject he can sink his teeth into for an entire meal. But finally when the fortune cookies are set down between them, she says, "The avalanche was so loud, I thought it would fill the entire valley. I didn't know how far we had to run to be safe."

Her husband nods solemnly, pours himself some more tea, pours some for her. She wishes he'd say something. She knows she talks too much. A person ought to say something once and be done with it. What's the use of talking a thing to death? But it's unnerving that he won't respond when she talks about things that are important to her. In the face of this, the need to talk builds perversely, until sometimes she wishes she could fling herself down and scream just to release the tension that swells inside like an unborn child. She would like to cure herself of this, would like to be more like him: contained and silent. Now that Drew has moved away and Susan is applying for teaching jobs, the need for this has become imperative. One ought to be able to be alone with one's experiences.

She watches Peter break into the cookie and pull out the little white slip. He reads the foolish aphorism aloud, another custom, but his eyes are focused somewhere far away. She studies the way he runs his tongue across his lips as if he's someone she'll need to keep in her memory.

She usually takes Robert to the mountains on Sundays, but this time she takes him to a show at the Aviary in the park. At this show, a crow retrieves a dime. Parrots say a few words. A crippled eagle glares from his perch like an angry old man. He tries to spread his wings, but he can't fly because, as the keeper explains, he was shot by hunters. A cockatoo is released from a cage to fly in a shocking whir of whiteness to the top of a tree and back to its keeper's hand. All this makes Margaret want to cry a little, and she hopes that Robert now understands the importance of birds.

This much she's been able to offer since the beginning: to show this child a world outside the dark living room. In that living room, he seems to belong only to Peter, and the two of them huddle together as though the world outside has been destroyed in a war and they are the only ones still alive. When Robert is sick, it's Peter who sleeps with him on the sofa, with the TV on for comfort, who holds him when he cries and cries for his mother, the mother consigned to that ruined world. What Margaret does is to insist on a world outside that still lives, and so she can't really belong with them. But she and Robert nearly died in the mountains and have come back together: bone of her bone, blood of her blood.

She thinks about this, and a few nights later after Robert has gone to bed, she lays her hand on the book her husband is reading and says, "I want to adopt Robert."

His eyes flick to hers. "That's very nice," he says, and removes her hand from his book.

Not long after, they have dinner with friends. She waits until the coffee, but then she tells them about the avalanche: "It was so hard to run! The snow under our feet was like old cheese and we kept falling through it." She avoids her husband's eyes, which would be angry or bored and goes on because she can't help it: "And Robert, he didn't want to run. He didn't understand the danger, so I had to push him."

Her husband says, "Yeah I bet." Their friends look at him curiously, for his tone is sharp. She thinks to ask him just what he means, thinks better of it. And besides, it's clear what he means: he sees her as being pushy. This makes her curl her fist to her chest against an old and mindless fear. As everyone has said since time immemorial, there is nothing more dreadful, more unsexed, than a pushy woman.

And so she waits a few more nights until they're alone together in the car to say again what's pressing inside her like a new story: "I love Robert as my own child. I've just discovered this. That's why I want to adopt him."

"Rita will never consent," he says.

"I think she would if you talked to her."

"Where would I find her?"

"But the courts would award this in her absence, yes? After a certain time?" She feels a moment of guilt towards Rita, but then the hawklike keenness of a mother sweeps into her, and she adds, "I think Robert would be comforted, knowing I'm that committed."

They sit there in the car, a silence humming between them like stirred-up dust. Then, though she knows she's saying too much, she says "You'd have to let the judge know that this is something you really want, too."

"Of course, I want it too," he says. But he says it without the press of someone who really wants.

The next morning she has a dream that she lives in a house made of blue glass. This glass is oddly rippled. Ducks flying south mistake it for a body of water, crash into the glass and die. As with so many of her dreams lately, she can't shake the feeling of it even after she's long awake. She cuts Robert's hair that evening. He's learning not to wriggle so much and she's figured out how to feather it so it tapers to the ends. She leaves a longer lock in the back and thinks he looks sort of stylish. Soon he'll want to go to a barber like the other boys and she'll need to find some other way to be useful.

She wonders why she is finding it so hard to feel useful. She moved to this part of the country in order to climb mountains and be a strong, outdoors sort of person. After a while, this seemed not enough reason for a life, as if important parts of herself weren't being used, and so with Peter and Robert she hoped to become someone useful and unselfish. She whisks the back of Robert's neck with a Kleenex and gathers up clumps of hair into a paper bag. "Go look at yourself in the mirror," she says, "and tell me if you like it." Perhaps, she thinks, I am not unselfish at all, because I want so much for him and Peter to like what I do.

Come Sunday again, she has a plan, which only dimly makes sense to her. They'll all three of them go to the site of the avalanche. Robert likes the idea so much that Peter is forced to agree to come along. Peter prefers to spend his weekend days at home and is disturbed by her restless wanting to be outside. "You're always poised for flight," he often says. "You make me nervous." But today, he's coming along and she's happy, sings a few songs, skips ahead of them on the path to the waterfall like a child. Robert catches up to her, takes her hand, skips along with her. Then they stop and stare at the rock at the base of the cliff where they narrowly escaped being crushed by some fifteen feet of snow.

The rock is bare. In these few short weeks, all the snow has melted. Now Peter will never believe her. She wants to find something to make this avalanche real to him. Can people insist, she wonders, that what they experience must be shared and given its due importance?

"Come, let's climb beside the falls. I'll show you where the avalanche came from." Without looking back, she wedges a foot into a crack and pulls herself up on the granite. She climbs swiftly and easily, lets herself go loose at the waist and hopes that Peter will notice the sway of her hips. She's careful to avoid the wet slippery rocks at the edge of the waterfall. She swerves into an outcrop of scrub pine, then out again onto the granite face. Finally she reaches the cirque, where the granite stops and the mountain sucks itself into an enormous bowl below the peak. Patches of snow are studded with small black rocks like a night sky on a negative. Threads of snowmelt wander and then merge above the channel of the waterfall. Nothing remains to show that an avalanche has let fall its terrible weight.

She turns around, about to apologize to Peter, but he hasn't followed her. She climbs heavily to a patch of snow, lies down and sweeps her arms and legs back and forth to make an angel. The snow has hardened into sharp crystals and now rasps against her bare arms like something that could wear her down. She lies there for a long time, feeling the cold seep into her. Of course, Peter hasn't followed. Robert is with them. The climb would be too dangerous for the child, and she hadn't thought of that. The mother-bond, perhaps, was merely a dream. And Peter. He'll never follow her anywhere, no matter what. Their marriage is over, has been over for a long time. The shame of this, the waste, and her own uselessness lift her up into a fist and squeeze her chest as if to crush her breath away. She can't imagine how she'll bring herself to leave them.

Then she begins the long, careful climb back down, which is always harder. Somewhere on the way down, it comes to her: the birds are Western Finches. She'll have to remember to tell Robert.

Cornbelt Blues

The ripening corn closed in on the highway like steep riverbanks through which the August heat flowed, swampy and thick with chaff and exhaust. The three of them had floated this river from the Rocky Mountains clear to the straining heart of the cornbelt. "My little lifeline," Drew would say from time to time, stroking the blue-gray fur of the cat, who was a wonder, because he liked to travel. The horse, likewise, traveled serenely, out of sight and silent in the trailer behind.

Farmers and other right-minded Americans would see this corn as beautiful. When Drew looked across the acres from a rise in the road what she saw was not beauty but a dull gold-tipped burr, like the haircut of a Marine or a very obedient child. Sometimes, instead of corn, there were soybeans. And now and then a silo, a halfhearted barn, a farmhouse, some tired-looking trees.

She let her mouth sag open, passively taking in the thump of the tires, and the heat, which clamored like blood beating around an angry wound. She willed herself to stay awake. She'd fallen asleep at the wheel twice the day before, awakened with a jolt in the passing lane, and it had not yet been noon. She'd also developed a mysterious vertigo, so if she turned her head too quickly, everything started to spin. The cat lay like a rope across her lap, stretched full length at half-twist, panting in the heat. Bill shifted in the trailer and she knew he was sighing, as horses do when there is nothing else for it.

Drew spoke the silly phrases that are the luxury of those without a human audience: "My little lifeline. Why are we doing this? He doesn't want us to come." Her hand rested on the panting cat. "It's crazy."

What do you do when you aren't sure you're wanted by the person you love? You do the crazy thing and insist that you're needed. You think that you have been self-centered and too easily hurt. You do whatever's hardest, because that will burn out of you all that makes you unworthy. The canyons of corn are as dark and impersonal as the inner city. You drive in deeper because you want to be brave. You drive into the heavy heat like a dumb animal, a brainstem, everything else peeled away like paint in a fire.

You stop trying to make sense of things, but you see things in your memory. See, for instance, that red-rock ranch in Wyoming when you held down a ewe while the rancher pulled the lamb out of her. See the arm of the deliverer covered with water and blood, the longing in his dark eyes, and feel your own mother-fist clenching and unclenching low in the belly. See the jealous eyes of the rancher's daughter, who wants her daddy to herself. And see yourself go back home to your husband, whose green eyes are as distant as stars as he tells you he's taken a job in central Illinois.

"You can have the mountains," Barry said. He swept wide his arms as if he were, in fact, giving them to her. "It's a great opportunity, this job. It doesn't matter where." He had to fly to Illinois immediately, some special research project that needed programming, some enormous grant, a whole staff to train. She could arrange to ship his things to him, and later she could drive the truck out herself. "Of course I want you to come," Barry said, putting on his perplexed-eyebrow look when she'd tried to force the moment to its crisis. "You're my wife, after all."

Yes, after all. What did it mean to be a wife? Once she'd thought she'd never consent to be a wife. But he'd persisted so. Such earnestness! Such need! His eyes were sad. His hands, a reaper's. Oh come with me to live in the mountains! I'd be lost without you! She hadn't known until then that something crouching inside her like a runaway child had waited a long time for exactly that persistence. This runaway had risen up like a tyrant and decided it was time to go home, commanded that she take up this marriage like the thread of an old forgotten story.

The odd thing was that once she'd married him and moved with him to the mountains, that need of his had vanished. The child-tyrant screamed and arched her back against the pain, then settled back into the old hiding place—but not entirely. Drew sold the horse he'd given her as a wedding present, an impossible animal, all beauty, no common sense, and bought Bill, a horse that could think. He'd been abandoned by his owners, came cheap, came into her life when she needed him most. Then she adopted the cat, who'd come to their door as a mewling stray. She lavished her love on the animals instead of the man. Barry was a brilliant man; he could tell you all there was to know about computers. He could not, however, talk about what had come between them. Whatever it was, it added up to this: he no longer needed her.

Then came the month she spent at an artist's colony in Wyoming when she thought about leaving Barry to be with the dark-eyed rancher. But she believed that marriage was not something you let go of lightly, and she went back to her husband, not ready to give up. That was when he told her he'd accepted a job far away from the mountains.

"Stay," her good friends said. They didn't like Barry. Susan said, "You need someone who believes in love." Margaret pointed to the mountains and said, "You need this."

But she couldn't answer them except to say, "I have to see it through."

"Will you take your animals?" they asked. They did not add the obvious, that Barry didn't like her animals.

Up the next little rise, the engine started to miss, a drag in the river, like sandbars. Drew shook herself out of the waking sleep of long-distance driving, clamped her mouth shut. She sat up straighter, checked the gauges on the dashboard, which answered her nothing. The mystery of engines was as unfathomable as love. Something about gasoline getting it on with oxygen. Gaps now in that story, but why? The cat leaped from her lap onto her shoulder. She reached up and thrust it back down roughly. "No kitty. Not now." The horse did something in the trailer that made a dull thud, rocked them a little.

She was angry. Barry ought to be with her. This was too hard. In this heat, stranded, they'd be in trouble. Bill would have to be unloaded, since there'd be no breeze to keep him cool inside the trailer. A passing truck might scare him; he might run off. No, they simply had to make it to the next exit.

And so they did. The gas station man was burly, his skin and hair a dusty dark with years of oil and grease. His nose was flat at the bridge as if he'd broken it once. He heard her out, shook his head sympathetically, said it was most certainly a vapor-lock, for the temperature outside was over a hundred and so no wonder. There was nothing for it, he said, but to hole up in a motel until darkness came and it was cool enough to drive.

Drew sighed. "I'm towing a horse. He'll have to be stabled."

The gas-station man took off his visor cap, ran his hands through his hair. "My wife. She had a horse. It died. You can use the pasture."

Drew imagined a faded woman gazing across the empty pasture, her lips pressed together, her eyes sunk in from all that sun, all that loss. How would the poor woman take to a strange horse where the other used to be? But she was too tired to think, so she said, "All right."

The gas station man, who introduced himself as "just Link," hung a "closed" sign in the window and drove ahead of her to his home. He helped Drew unload Bill, opened the pasture gate, showed her where the water bucket was. The horse snatched a few mouthfuls of grass, sniffed at some piles of old manure, then noticed he was free, tossed his head and plunged across the field, twisting and bucking. Drew turned to fetch water, some hay, and saw a girl of about twelve, barefoot, wearing shorts and a halter. She had that flat place on the bridge of her nose, that dusty look of hair not quite black, skin not often washed. But her eyes were intelligent and large, a stunning shade of blue.

"Hi there, darling," the man said, and reached for the child. The girl twisted away, darted around him to stand beside Drew.

"My mom isn't here," she said.

"I'm sure she'll be home soon," said Drew, disliking the whine in the girl's voice.

"No she won't." The girl turned away from them, walked toward the house, which stood in the shade of some trees. The girl's legs were thin but starting to show maturing muscle at the calves. Drew watched her until she disappeared into the house. She looked inquiringly at the man who called himself Link.

He shrugged. "That's my daughter Jody. Betty'll be back. She'll think twice."

She finished getting water and hay for her horse and said, "I'll go find a motel now."

"There ain't one."

"But you said..."

"There's one ten miles south, but your truck won't make it that far until its cool."

The girl Jody came back out and handed Drew a glass of lemonade. "Thought you'd be thirsty," she said. She looked up with those surprising eyes and said, "Come inside out of the sun. Please."

"You're welcome to stay here," Link said. "I'll wake you up so you can catch the cool time." He cocked his thumb toward his truck. "Got to go back to work now. Be home kind of late. She'll tell you where to find things." He walked a few steps, stopped, turned and said, "You can bring that cat inside."

Drew didn't like the idea of going into a strange house without a woman around, but she was too tired to think of what else to do. "All right. Thank you very much." She wiped the sweat around her mouth with her hand and gulped down the lemonade.

The farmhouse was cool and neat. One wall of the kitchen was covered with cross-stitched samplers with pious sayings like, "Abide with Me." The girl was at the sink washing a head of lettuce. "I'll make you a sandwich. Tomatoes fresh from the garden. I grew them myself."

The cat was sniffing into the corners, his way of taking in a place. He'd be fine, as he always was. Jody came over to where Drew sat at the kitchen table and set a sandwich and another glass of lemonade down in front of her. "I had a cat once," she said, "but she got run over. You could see where the tire went."

"I'm sorry." Drew wasn't very hungry, but she bit into the sandwich, found it good. The girl stood and watched her eat.

"My mom had a horse once. It died."

"Your father told me. That's sad." She felt sleepy, wondered if it would be rude to ask to take a nap. It might be wise to sleep now and leave as soon as the sun went down. But the girl sat down at the table and leaned her chin on her hands as if to study Drew more closely.

"You look sort of like my mom," she said.

"I'm sorry your mom isn't here," Drew said. And she realized she was sorry, perhaps because of the time she'd spent imagining the woman.

"She went to stay with her parents." The girl said this matter-of-factly, but Drew thought she saw a flash of worry in her eyes.

They sat a while not saying anything. Drew wanted to wash her face and lie down. She began to rise from her chair, but the girl reached to her and touched her arm. "Help me," she said.

"What?"

"Help me." The girl pulled her hands into a knot in her lap.

"Help you how?"

She pointed to the back of the house. "Make him happy."

Drew felt the dizziness coming on again. She sat back down and gripped the edge of the table. "I'm sorry. I don't know what you mean."

The girl looked up at Drew, her eyes full of tears. "I don't want to make him happy anymore."

Drew reached her hand to the middle of the table to keep it from spinning. "Well, I'm not likely to make him happy!" She tried to make this sound jovial, like a self-deprecating joke, as a way to cover up the sudden stab of shock. She did not want to get to the heart of this exchange. She could not deal with this from a vortex of exhaustion and dizziness.

The girl stared at her for a long time. Then she said, "Never mind." She knelt down on the floor and called to the cat. "Pretty kitty! Pretty kitty!" She smiled up at Drew. "You've got a nice kitty," she said, as though nothing had been said at all.

Drew rose from the table and found that she was trembling at the knees. "I've got to sleep a while. I'll leave when the sun goes down."

The girl looked up at her from where she sat on the floor, the cat curled in her arms. "All right. I'll have some dinner ready."

Drew tried to stay awake so she could think about what the girl had said, but she fell into the sleep of the dead. When she woke up, it was nearly dark, and the room whirled around as if she were in the middle of a tornado. It wouldn't be safe to drive, but it wouldn't be safe here, either. There was a soft knock on the door. Drew sat up quickly and the tornado turned on edge, came at her sideways. The girl turned on the light and came into the room with a tray of food. "I thought you'd be wanting to get up soon," she said. "My dad isn't home yet. It's all right."

Drew tried to sit up straighter and groaned against a wave of nausea.

"You're sick," the girl said.

"Maybe. I think all I can eat are soda crackers. Do you have any?"

The girl came back with a box of crackers. "Here, keep the whole box if it helps." She sat down on the edge of the bed. She'd combed her hair and put on clean clothes. "Take me with you," she said. "Please."

Drew felt a sudden rush of affection for the girl and wanted to gather her into her arms, but her arms stayed helplessly at her sides. She tried to think.

"I can't stay here one more night." The girl's blue eyes grew wide with something like fear.

"Where do you want to go?"

"To my mother. Like I said, she's staying with my grandparents just a few towns over."

"Your father won't take you there?" Drew bit her lower lip, thinking that of course he wouldn't take her, unless she was misunderstanding the girl completely. Perhaps she should question the girl to pin down exactly what was going on. But she did not feel clear enough in her mind to do this, and she thought it might be something better handled by an expert. What would Barry say? She couldn't imagine. She could barely call up his face in her memory. Perhaps he'd suggest taking the girl to the police, but Drew had read somewhere that police weren't always understanding about this sort of thing.

Drew knew she couldn't live with herself if she didn't try to help the girl, so she finally said, "I'll take you to your mother, but you must call your father as soon as you get there."

The girl took a deep breath and said, "Thank you."

Bill did not want to be caught. He whirled away from Drew in the twilight and circled back, ran off again. Drew wanted to hurry, and it was all she could do to walk around the pasture acting like she didn't care, which is what you have to do with a horse. Finally the horse succumbed to the lure of a bucket of oats and let himself be loaded into the trailer. The cat was put into his carrier. The girl clambered into the seat beside her carrying a small suitcase and the box of crackers. "Let's get out of here," she said. "I left Daddy a note."

"Which way?" Drew asked.

"South, I think. Not very far."

After they'd driven for a while, the girl said, "Please don't tell the police. I don't think they'd believe me. They'd send me home or to one of those special schools." She was silent a while. "And if they did believe me, I'd get my daddy into trouble."

Drew knew this was probably true. She needed more rest, time to think, time for the world to set itself level again. She could drive only if she set her eyes dead ahead. If she looked into the rearview mirror, the world began to spin and she felt she might faint. She wondered if she were indeed ill, though this was unlike any sickness she'd ever had. It might not be safe to drive very far tonight. The cat cried in its carrier, wanting to be on her lap.

Linton proved to be just one exit away. As she navigated the off-ramp she asked Jody which way to turn for her grandparent's house.

"I don't know."

"What do you mean, you don't know?"

The girl shrugged. "We don't visit there very often. Daddy always drives and I don't pay attention."

A new wave of dizziness overtook Drew. She was afraid to drive much longer, sure that she'd make a silly mistake, attract the attention of a cruiser for some moving violation. "How about if we find a motel so I can have someplace to sleep after I drop you off? I'll look up your grandparents' address from there and then call them for directions. What's their last name?"

"Actually, it's sort of complicated. You see, they aren't my mom's real parents and they have a different name than hers."

"Which is?"

"I can't remember."

Well. In any case, if Drew didn't get some more sleep and get over this dizziness, nothing would get solved. She checked into the town's motel, tethered the horse to the trailer at edge of the parking lot, threw him some hay, carried the cat and the litterbox into their room. She and the girl sat facing each other on their respective beds. Drew could think of nothing to say.

Jody smiled at her and said, "It's all right. I left Daddy a note, remember?" Drew was unable to keep her eyes open any longer, and the two of them slept the whole night through.

The next morning Drew awakened with a start, sat up, reeling with vertigo, and saw the girl curled up in the other bed with her arms pressed around a pillow. The cat slept across her feet. Drew woke her up and said urgently, "You must call your father right away." The girl looked unhappy, but she obediently dialed, got no answer. "Try the gas station." Drew said. But Jody shook her head and said, "He doesn't go in this early. He must be out somewhere." Drew sank back into her pillows and regretted everything she'd ever done. It occurred to her to call her husband, but she couldn't imagine how she'd explain or how she'd face his anger at her foolishness.

Finally she opened the phone book and located a doctor who could see her immediately. She left Jody and the cat in the room, gave Bill a flake of hay, and walked the few blocks to the doctor. It was a great effort not to stagger, for every few steps the world began to turn on end.

"Am I very sick?" she asked the doctor, and he said, "Sick enough, especially for someone on the road. You have an inner ear infection." He gave her a shot of antibiotics and a patch to wear that was supposed to stop the dizziness. His kindness made her want to weep, and it occurred to her how much she felt like a little girl herself.

She took Jody out to eat. The girl wolfed down scrambled eggs, three donuts and two glasses of milk. Drew munched on soda crackers, and said, "Now, look. Either we find your mother or we go to the police. Or we drive back to your father's."

Jody's face crumpled. "Please," she said. "Keep me with you a little longer. I keep trying to remember the name."

Drew and the girl took Bill for a walk along the road. He pranced on the leadline, overjoyed to be moving again. Soon his coat took on a damp sheen from the heat. The corn grew right up to the edge of the ditches, so tall it shut out the horizon. Between the ditch and the road were wildflowers an astonishing shade of blue. Jody was easy to be with. The whine had gone out of her voice and she walked alongside the horse and spoke to it in low tones, saying, "Them cornflowers are pretty. Don't you tramp on them. Be soft now. That truck won't run you over. That's it. Be soft." Drew smiled, liking her way with an animal.

When they got back to the motel and Bill was safely tethered to the trailer, Drew lay down on the bed, thinking she'd take a quick nap and then it would be time to act decisively. Jody curled up on the other bed, and the cat leaped into the crook of her arm. Nothing about this seemed quite real to Drew. She wasn't dizzy anymore, but the world had taken on a dreamlike cast in the hazy heat. She liked it here in this town where time seemed to have stopped many years ago. Maybe the two of them could live like this a while, as if they were passengers aboard a ship cut off from the world, not having to deal with anything much at all. She couldn't remember a time when she'd been this tired.

When she awakened it was nearly dusk. Jody was asleep, her dusty-dark hair spread out, the cat curled up against her. Drew thought the girl slept an unusual amount for someone who wasn't sick, but then, she might be doing another sort of healing. Drew stood over her and touched her hair, thinking it could use a washing. She decided she'd buy something for them to eat. It would be expensive to eat another meal in a restaurant. And then she must get Jody to call her father. By now, he might have the police looking.

She left a note for Jody and left for the grocery store, which was on the other side of town. She still felt shaky from her illness and there was no reason to hurry, so she walked slowly, taking in the character of the town. The houses were nearly all white frame, probably a hundred years or so old. Most of the people she saw were old. This was the sort of place young people would leave as soon as they could.

The store was a small supermarket with dust on the shelves. It was a kind of luxury to amble down the aisles and take a long time to decide what to buy. She bought a box of donuts, some sandwich fixings, some lemonade, a bottle of shampoo, and food for the cat. She was happy, and it occurred to her that she hadn't been happy like this for a long time.

On the way back to the motel she stopped on a little rise in the road to watch the sun go down. It sank clear to the horizon, just like on the ocean, bleeding at the edges like an overstrained heart. It came to her then that she wasn't in a hurry to be with Barry again. Why should she trade this simple happiness for living with someone who didn't need her? Maybe tomorrow she'd call the dark-eyed rancher in Wyoming, even if his daughter didn't like her. Maybe the courts would let her keep Jody. And maybe the rancher's daughter would like Jody for a friend, even a sister. Drew began walking again, imagining the delight in Jody's eyes when she pulled out the donuts.

The door to the motel room was partly open, light spilling from it like water tossed from a bucket. The cat ran up to her out of the twilight. She scooped it into her arms and went inside, feeling heavy and afraid. On the rumpled bed was a note. "My daddy found me," it said. "He didn't call the police. Don't worry. My mother's back. P.S. The name is Peterson."

What do you do now? You close the door and put down what you're carrying, sit down on the bed, and have an excellent cry. You cry for the girl, whose mother probably won't solve things with her pious sayings, even if she stays. You cry for lambs that have a hard time being born, and for all the stray cats and all the abandoned horses. And you cry for yourself and the way you never really help anyone very much, even though that's what people seem to want from you. And then you gather up your animals and your things and get back on the road.

The corn folds in on the road like a blanket and you know that even when it's dark the cornflowers are growing and there's some right place to go to, once you figure out where it is.

Pete's Rock

I'm married to a woman who ties excellent knots. You will understand the importance of this when I explain that I'm a construction carpenter by trade—slam-bam framing, overnight condos, fast-food joints. The foreman fires you if you get careful and slow. What makes me feel good about my life is not, therefore, my work, but the fact that I'm a rock climber. And for that, you've got to have your knots down, starting with the water knot, which is how you tie on your harness. A harness is a rigmarole of webbing that goes around your hips and is secured at the waist by a deceptively simple unity of two half-knots that must mesh exactly: the water knot. The rope is tied into the harness with a bowline and is what keeps you from certain death if you fall. Count on it: sooner or later you fall.

Another way I get to feel good about my life is the tower I'm building on our house. I bought a crummy little shack on the edge of the north foothills, tore off half the roof, and I'm going up two stories for a view of the mountains and light for Susan to paint by. She's always worrying about light: "This light is too yellow, George," she says. "The shadows are wrong, I can't even see what I'm feeling."

Who can hear such things and not want to make it better? I'm giving Susan all the light she'll ever need. I'm still working on the first story up, but even from there you can see the whole sweep of the valley, the rim of the south mountains some hundred miles away. I'm so happy to be living here after all those years in Brooklyn, tears almost come to my eyes. On top of the first story will be a second story, which will be Susan's studio. Sometimes Susan is crouched next to me, feeding nails, measuring out plywood. She says she likes to work with me, but I think it isn't going to be enough.

I've never met a person so sad as Susan. A song came on the radio while we were setting the boards on the new floor, a country song about nature being brought to her knees and can't we please leave a little blue window in the sky. That song put her into a fit of crying. But she smiled at me through the hair blown over her face. She rocked her lovely round hips over her knees, and said, "It's a good kind of crying. Don't look so scared." It scared me anyway. If I were to let things get to me the way she does, my hammer hand would be too heavy to raise above my head. On climbs I'd be pinned to the rock, unable to move either up or down.

Even so, I feel things getting to me a little more each day. Susan says the hammer calluses on my hands scrape her skin, but I tell her it's these same calluses that pay for this tower, pay for most everything we have. Sometimes it seems the more I do for her, the less she wants me. And sometimes I wish she would do little things for me, like come out of the kitchen, which temporarily doubles as her studio, and move close to me, brush her white fingers against my face. My mother used to tiptoe into my room and bring me warm milk. She'd touch my forehead and say, "Try not to make him angry," and for a while it would seem so simple a thing. After I turned ten, I never cried, no matter what, except a few years later when my parents died.

On a good day I can lead a 5.9 pitch. I've done all the big walls around here with Ian—not big by Yosemite standards, but the Black Warrior up the Canyon is a respectable thousand feet of water-streaked granite. Ian was my serious climbing partner. He and I usually climbed alone, but sometimes he invited Susan along, or a whole group. He's moving to Alaska because, he says, he's used up all the challenges here. His hair is thick and black and his body is stripped down to lean essentials. The need for new mountains keeps him restless. For me, it's enough being here. Moving out West to take up climbing is the best thing I ever did, that, and marrying Susan, who is the only woman I've loved and who once caught me in a twenty-foot lead fall.

She and I were climbing Pete's Rock, a big mound of quartzite set into the east foothills off the Boulevard. Pete's Rock is, in fact, where we met. I was bouldering along the lower ten feet of the rock, practicing traverses. She was in a University phys. ed. rock climbing class. Right away I noticed her shiny brown hair falling over her eyes and her hips that rocked like a cradle when she walked. We got to talking, arranged to meet and do a little climbing together. You could call Pete's rock the foundation of our marriage. A holy thing, marriage, though I will never say this to Susan because she doesn't believe in God. Ian told me that hidden high on this rock are ancient Indian petroglyphs—another holy thing—but because the climb to them is difficult and because they are hidden, he says, almost no one knows. I haven't told Susan about the petroglyphs, I don't know why.

Pete's Rock has big yellow numbers painted on it to indicate the official climbs. I can't imagine who would do such a thing; it's nothing like art. That day we were going to try number 11 at about the center, a one-pitch climb like the others. It had an overhang midway, but I was getting pretty good and I was bored with leading the easier stuff. I anchored Susan to a rock facing Pete at the base, tied the rope into her harness, into mine, made sure she'd looped the rope into the stitch plate and had herself braced. I put on my rack and walked to the base of the climb, clanking like a tower full of dead bells. A rack is a collection of metal chocks and nuts of various shapes and sizes hung on loops of narrow rope. It's a heavy load, but it saves your life.

I called out the ritual "Climbing!" and was on my way. It was easy at first: bucket handholds, footholds big enough for all my toes. Every six feet or so I rammed a chock into the narrow crack that ran up to the base of the overhang, clipped the rope into the caribiners attached to the rope slings. The idea is that if you fall, the hardware will jam into the crack, and the rope, caught at the caribiner, will hold you. You have to pay attention. It's easy to make a little mistake, and then you could die.

Just below the overhang was a horizontal crack into which I slammed a large hex nut. I yanked against it to make sure it would hold, yanked again, checked a few knots. I was at the crux and I wasn't sure what the move ought to be. Susan smiled up at me patiently. There's a lot of waiting in climbing. Sometimes when I wait for her to follow me up I think I'm going to lose my temper the way my father did, but this is something I swore I'd never do. Usually I just enjoy the view.

I couldn't see a sensible move. There was a problem with balance. To make it to the top of the overhang required that I defy gravity and push myself outward before I could find something above me to hold onto. This seemed to call for a lunge, and so I lunged, because it's important that I keep going, especially when I think of Ian, who glides up a 5.11 wall like a dancer. A mistake, the lunge. My hand slipped off the ledge, my feet kicked into nowhere, and my body flipped outward, tumbling me to a view of the sky, a rush in my chest like a whir of wings. I thought about how close I was to the ground. Would Susan be able to catch me before I hit bottom? Would the hex nut hold? Was my water knot tight enough? All of these things went through my mind, though much more quickly.

My rope doubled back on the rock like a safety pin, jerking me to a violent stop maybe five feet from the ground. I hung there without moving, at first because I'd lost my breath, and then because this was a momentous event and it made me feel kind of important. But Susan did not share the same sense of occasion, for she began yelling at me to get back on the rock because the pressure was, she said, cutting her in half. I saw her then, lifted off the ground against the webbing that held her to the tie-in, her waist pinched in like a Victorian lady. I managed to claw my way back onto the rock and take the pressure off, climbed down slowly, retrieved my hardware as I went, working slowly because I was shaking. I crumpled to the ground at the base, but then Susan said, "Help me get untied, my hands hurt like hell." Finally, we hugged each other, gathered up our equipment and loaded our gear in the back of Bertram, my wonderful squeaky Ford pickup, fire-engine red with old-fashioned woven straw seat covers. Buying this truck, more than anything, made me feel I'd really come to the West.

That night Susan and I made love like children let out of school, despite our scrapes and sore hands. We didn't climb Pete's rock after that, but moved on to the granite up the Canyon, the better rock, where the real climbs are. Susan and I don't do the big walls, but we enjoy the shorter climbs. Granite isn't as slippery as quartzite, and we get to do three, sometimes four pitches. When I see Susan rise up to me from under a belay ledge, the sweat shining like drops of gold on her face, her dark hair damp and curling at the edges, I feel like I'm king of the mountain, which I sort of am for that little moment. And then her hands push the rope to one side and reach up and cup the rock. Sometimes there's a little blood on the knuckles and her face crinkles up if the move is hard. She has beautiful pale hands like those small white moths you see in the woods. She can't muscle the moves the way a man can. She has had to learn to climb the better way, with a little finesse.

Susan thinks she has to prove that she's a brave person, but sometimes I want to say to her, "Stop! Save yourself for the baby!" Even so, I'm not unselfish enough to ask her to stop climbing with me, because I love those dizzy drops we look down at together. Most of all, I get to see myself as a patient man when I climb with her. This is important when all your life you've been afraid you'll end up like your father. And besides, there isn't any baby yet, maybe never will be.

With her beautiful white hands Susan paints watercolors so tender I could cry if I were the sort of person who cried. She's finishing up graduate school so she can get a university job teaching others how to paint. It's a calling, she says, a sacred obligation. Sometimes I think I'm not a good enough man for her.

What does it mean to be a good-enough man? I think it means to be sort of like a tree. You plant yourself in one place and let your woman blow at you like the wind and say to her: "I'll always be here." You have to let her pound you with her fists to try to make you soft or make you mean. You have to let her try to make you go away. But you just stand there, sure of yourself the way Ian is, but willing to stick around. And finally, she'll trust you and come to lie underneath you with her eyes full of sunlight and leaves.

But I think none of this will work. I wish my mother were still alive so I could ask what it was that kept her with my father even though he ground her down. I would ask her if I'm doing the right thing building this tower, if I shouldn't instead be taking Susan to Alaska or maybe Paris, or pretending I love another woman. It's a funny world because nothing you decide seems right or wrong; it seems only to work or not to work.

I am haunted by the thought of those petroglyphs hidden somewhere on Pete's Rock. I think I'm angry at the rock for pushing me off itself, want to cut it down to size, penetrate its secret place. And I keep thinking of those ancient Indians who got to live around here before the fast-food places and the condos. I think, too, of how I want Susan to look at me when her eyes stare in my direction—at me, and not at some far-away idea about a painting.

So today I don't want to work on the house, even though that's what I do on my days off. The sun touches the foothills like a mother's hand, and I need to be in a place where I can feel something like love. I say to Susan just as she's lifted up a can of nails, "I'm going to Pete's Rock today."

She wrinkles up her nose, says, "What on earth for?"

"It's going to be a surprise."

"You're going alone?" She sets the nails back down, touches my hand so lightly I might be imagining it. "Be careful."

My father liked to do surprises. When I was almost ten, I found the bicycle he was going to give me for my birthday. It was in the space between the furnace and the crawl space opening, not really hidden at all. A Schwinn racer, it was bright red and had the kind of horn you squeeze with a bulb. I stood for a long time staring at the bike, thinking how lucky I was. He came down the basement stairs, a man with quiet feet despite his size, and found me standing there. He grabbed my arm with his enormous hand, took off his belt. Afterwards he lifted up the bike, saying he was taking it back to the store. But on my birthday the bike was in the living room when I came downstairs for breakfast. I never knew what he was going to do. He worked in a bakery and his arms were white and plump like the dough he worked with his enormous hands. When I bake bread for Susan, I like to imagine that the flour is the good white part of a person that's there when all the stuff you're scared of has been burned away.

My mother was a tiny woman, fluttery and nervous. When my father was home, she was never still, but darted from room to room, picking things up, straightening pictures, hurrying upstairs, back down again. She died of cancer when she was only forty-five. A woman who thought a lot about God, she said the cancer was His anger because she hadn't been a good enough wife. I thought it was because she couldn't stand the weight of my father on her any longer; though it's funny, he died, too, of a heart attack, only a few years later. Toward the end I sometimes sat on the edge of his bed to keep him company. Once he grabbed my hand and squeezed so hard I thought the bones would crack. A person has to be there for someone, even if it means hurting a little.

I have this idea about Pete's. I'll do the easy hike up the back of the rock to the top and drive in a bolt. Then I'll rappel down, probably have to do some tricky traversing, but I'll find the petroglyphs and photograph them. I think this might impress Susan. She says I'm too dependent, never doing things by myself. She says, "You're always in my hair." And I can see how she'd like it if I weren't so tangled up in her.

I load my rope and harness into Bertram, stop by the climbing store for a bolt and hammer, go to Osco for one of those disposable cameras, with a flash in case the shadows are wrong, fill up the truck with gas, and head up to Pete's. Bertram stalls at a light, and when I get him going again, I pat the dash and say, "Hang in there, man, we're going to make it." A first truck can be almost like a person in your life.

I hammer the bolt into the top of Pete's at about dead center, thinking I can swing down a few feet, traverse to the right, then to the left, go down a few more feet, traverse right, left, and so on, until I find the petroglyphs. I'll be a fine-toothed rock-comber, a man on his first solo, adventurous as Ian. I'm carrying a spare sling, so I tie on a prussik—a brilliant little knot Ian showed me once that jams up tight on the rope if you put weight on it. After lowering myself a few feet I tighten the prussik and let go of the rope so I can traverse using both hands. It is harder to move sideways on the rock than to climb up. Much of this is in the mind, because you know that if you fall, you're going to pendulum, maybe get kind of banged up.

I hitch down another bounce of rappel, traverse right, traverse left, haven't found a thing. The sun is getting low. I have the camera in a clean chalk bag and it thumps against my hip when I move. The air is humid for this part of the country and sweat keeps getting into my eyes and making my hands slippery. Gnats buzz around my ears. I'm getting tired.

Ian told me about someone who'd climbed solo, gotten himself into a hornet's nest, tried to escape on a rappel, had fallen and died. Ian enjoys stories that remind him of the danger of what he does. I would like to have his kind of courage, except that I think such a zest for danger might keep me from enjoying things, like coming home every day to someone with hips that hold me like a hanging nest. I think Ian is a lonely person. He might even be a sad person in those moments when he isn't grabbing at a 5.10 layback. Which might be why he asked Susan along on so many climbs this past year. We went together to the City of the Rocks, where the granite pokes up for miles like those towers in Iran, and Susan got stuck on a move for almost an hour. And there was the climb in October that took some eight hours because the rocks were covered with ice. I'd forgotten to bring gloves. On the razorback ridge I thought my hands were going to fall off from the cold. Ian looked like a God that day in the high foggy sunlight, and when the sun backlighted him so you couldn't see his face, it was as if he'd become one of those granite spires.

I lower myself down to a ledge and find myself staring at the scaly yellow number 11. I'm on top of the overhang that threw me off the rock. There's a moment of guilt, as if I've cheated, but then I get hold of a peaceful sense of the rightness of things. I give myself a little time to enjoy the view, which is nothing less than the entire sweep of the valley clear to the Oquirrah mountains in the west. The sun burns low and bronze across the autumn-red foothills, and for the millionth time since I'd moved out west, I say out loud, "Thank you, God, for letting me live here." I put it like that in case my mother's god is still around, and because such happiness seems to call for the biggest giver you can think of.

When I finally get around to studying the rock, I notice a crack to the left so wide a limber person like Ian could squeeze into it, even chimney up a few feet. This crack isn't visible from the base of Pete's, but only from this special spot at the top of the overhang. I peer inside and think I see pale markings that could be petroglyphs—the spikes of a sun, perhaps, the arc of a running deer. I can't be sure. I wish I'd brought a flashlight. I stand pressed into that crack for a long time, breathing in the memory of the person who came here centuries before the condos and the fast-food places, that slender man who braved the slippery quartzite to find this secret place to write his stories or to talk to his God or whatever he did. I can't bear to think that lives don't count for something. A person has to be remembered. You have to find something a person left behind, touch it, breathe into it, and then he's never really dead.

Finally, I aim the camera into the crack and flash through the entire roll at different angles. I do this with a guilty conscience, for I've heard that primitive people believe you take a slice of their souls when you photograph them, and I wonder if I'm killing off whatever spirit might still be hanging around. But the overriding thing is that I want to show the pictures to Susan. The surprise I'll give her will be the pictures proving that I've done this without telling her beforehand. And besides, only from the photos can I be certain whether I've really found the petroglyphs or just seen some random scratches in the rock.

I slip the spent camera back into the chalk bag and begin to rappel straight down. It's like those dreams where you keep going back to the same scary places: the crack underneath the overhang where I'd jammed the hex nut, the bucket handholds, the slick cups for my toes, the thin vertical crack where I'd placed the chocks. At one point I forget to loosen the prussik and I hang myself up, so I let go of the rope for a moment and let the prussik hold me, just to feel again what it's like to be caught and held above the ground. At the base of Pete's, I untie the rope and pull it hissing into a heap at my feet. I think of Susan and me tearing at each other, rolling around and moaning and laughing, her touch like a shock of mountain rain and then like a flame low in the belly.

I dump my rope into Bertram's bed, untie the chalk bag with the camera in it and carefully place it in the glove compartment. When I start the truck, I smell smoke. I drive for a few yards, thinking the smoke must be someone's illegal campfire, but then I realize the smoke is here, inside the cab. I pull over fast, get out, and yank back the old straw-woven seat. Smoke billows out, right next to the gas tank. I stand foolishly, wondering how such a fire could start, think of wires shorting, a dropped cigarette, except that I don't smoke. Then I think of my rope, which cost a lot of money and saved my life. I slam the door shut, grab the rope out of the pickup bed, and run for my life along the shoulder of the Boulevard, waiting to hear the gas tank blow.

After what seems like a long time of running, I stop and look back. Bertram is in flames. This feels like the anger of God, maybe the God of the man whose soul I've just stolen. The gas tank isn't going to blow, I realize, because I just filled it today, so there weren't any fumes inside. A man driving a black Blazer stops and says he'll call the fire department. Cars crawl around the burning truck. The flames roar higher and yank at the darkening sky like they're trying to pull it down on top of us all.

I need Susan next to me now. We'd hold hands, turn our faces bravely up to the fire, and say, "Oh wow," a few times, even cry a little together, who knows? But she isn't here. She's never here anymore.

I see as clearly as a dream the party Susan and I went to a few weeks ago. It was in a backyard full of mostly her friends, and I wanted to leave. Then Ian arrived. He walked along the edge of the lawn, close to the late-blooming roses, his steps tender, almost hurting, like a cat's. He came up to us and said, "I'm leaving for Alaska in a few days. I've come to say good-bye."

Ian was always the one to go up first, the rope trailing from his harness like an afterthought. He'd smile down from a finger-jam and say, "Another epic adventure, yes!" And Susan glowing like a new sky, going for moves she'd never try with just me. Should I let this bother me, or should I let it go? If you say something out loud, then it takes on a life of its own, gets bigger, takes over everything else. And, besides, it's over now. He's gone. And I'm here, a man who maybe isn't good enough. My fist is curled into my palm. Bertram isn't done with burning yet. He sends up showers of sparks like signals for help.

It isn't until after the fire engines have come and sprayed too little too late the black curling beast that used to be Bertram, after the wrecker has taken him away, and after some nice person has driven me home, that I remember the camera in the glove compartment. I won't get to know if I'd found the petroglyphs. Susan won't see the evidence of this solo journey I'll never have the heart to take again.

Susan doesn't cry when I tell her what happened to Bertram, but she scolds me for risking my life to save the rope. She says it's important to know what caused the fire so it won't happen again, but I think that one way or another things happen again no matter how much you know. She asks me why on earth was I rappelling down Pete's rock, but something stops me from explaining. She reaches for me as if to comfort, but I pull my hands away, and knot them in my lap. I think of the calluses that could scrape her skin, and how even though my hands aren't especially big, they could hurt a person if I'm not careful. If I could cry, I would cry for these hands.

Wichita

Now the two of them walk silently in the chill of the morning. This silence is a little strained, but it gives them the time they need to settle themselves into this sudden meeting. Before Margaret can go somewhere else to start over, she knows she has to begin here, with Rita, in this place she loves to say out loud: Wichita.

Wichita is not only in the middle of the country, but it is where many things meet and cross each other. Two rivers converge here, the Big and Little Arkansas, and then go on their separate ways. And here is where the Great Plains end and the Southwest begins. The wind from the Gulf of Mexico and the wind from the Arctic also cross exactly here. Just to the west, the irrigation belt begins. Here, church congregations gather and pray for rain.

Margaret drove to Wichita straight through from Denver. The winds joined forces along the freeway like sullen gangs, rushed at the side of her car with sudden vicious swipes, tossed tumbleweeds under the wheels. Still she drove on. She didn't know why, but she had to see Rita right away. If nothing else, she's learned to listen to the part of her that says, "This is what you need to do." When she reached Wichita, she parked the car in an empty shopping center, slept a few hours, then called Rita.

Margaret and Rita are walking in Chisholm Creek Park to the north of the city. There are hiking trails in this park. They are paved, and they curve through fields of tall grass. Margaret thinks that this grass traces its origin to the grasses of the virgin prairie. There's a small excitement in this, a sense of history, of things kept alive. Now, in early March, the grasses are yellow and broken. Some of them have little knobs on the ends or starburst clusters of dried-out flowers. Perhaps what she is seeing are weeds, actually, not grasses at all. But before the farmers and the dust, the prairie must have been resplendent with weeds, too. She tries to make this interesting; she wants to enjoy this place for what it is. But she can't stop thinking of the place she has just left behind: mountains with rock walls flowing down like great frozen waterfalls, hiking trails that leave you breathless and your heart swooping like a sudden bird.

She darts a glance at Rita, has to look up a little because the other woman is tall. Rita's dark hair blows around her face, and she tosses her head like an impatient horse. She looks very much like Robert, but has Peter's round face and the nearly flat nose of a child, so the resemblance seems unreliable. Margaret never had many opportunities to look at Rita, who was always in a hurry when she came to the house. From the first, Margaret had a hunger to look at her, a kind of awe, because the woman was Robert's mother.

Margaret was Robert's stepmother, something altogether different. She still doesn't understand what stepmothers are supposed to be like, though she read books, joined a group, tried to talk it out with Peter, who found the subject painful, perhaps because he still loved Rita. Margaret wanted to be something more than dutiful to Robert. She wanted to find a bond, though just what sort of bond she wasn't clear. She took him places, got him out of the house. She took him on a sketching hike in the mountains.

They sat on a flat rock in the shade of a scrub pine, and she showed him what charcoal could do. Already showing signs of being a gifted artist, this child was driven to a perfection beyond his years. He fretted over a smudge, his voice rising to a wail: "I've made a mistake."

"Mistakes are good things for artists," she told him. "They let the drawing be interesting, not like a photo. Look. It's a good mistake." She pointed to the thicket of pine he was trying to capture. "Those trees do look sort of blurry, especially if you squint and look at them with artist's eyes." She scrunched up her face into an exaggerated squint to make him laugh. "With mistakes," she went on, "there's feeling in the picture."

He laughed as she'd hoped he would and asked her, his moon-round face leaning out into the sunlight, "There's such a thing as good mistakes?"

"Yes," she told him, "absolutely."

He carried that idea like a gift, squinted sometimes and said, "I've got artist's eyes," as if he knew his saying that was a gift to her. For seven years she lived with him. He tried to call her Mom. It started out as muh-muh-muh, his dark eyes darting to hers to see how she was taking it. She let him see her delight, but not, she hoped, so it was a pressure for more. Finally he came out with it. It made her absurdly happy. She felt the way a mother might: that tendency to brag to friends about him; to find other mothers to talk to about diet, TV, bedtimes; that funny ache on the insides of her arms for the pressure of his small body. The child could also drive her crazy sometimes, and they were reduced now and then to yelling fights that made Peter very angry at her.

"Peace and Quiet. Is that too much to ask?"

Father words. No one had yelled in her family. She thought it would be a healthy thing to shout a little now and then, have it out with the gusto of what felt like love. Better than the icy silences that surrounded her as a child with loneliness and worry. She has come to realize this: we overcorrect. We make mistakes. Not all mistakes can be seen with an artist's eye. Her mistakes, which she is not yet clear about, were bad enough that Peter has told her to get out of his life. He would not say why, just, "I'm unhappy. Sorry. It isn't going to work." Time enough later, he said, for drawing up the papers and such. For now, simply: "Go away from us." Margaret believes this could only happen to a person who has done something very wrong. It's as if marriage were some incomprehensible board game with rules that change with every move, a game she lost because of some unexplained and terrible incompetence. For Robert, the players are outside his control, yet he stands to lose the most.

Robert has this mother, his real one, Rita, for whom his loyalty is fierce and heartbreaking. She sees him maybe once a year, more when she lived out west. He never spent the night with her because she was not always reliable. Once, Peter had to call the police to get him out of her locked apartment when she'd passed out. "I couldn't wake her up,"

Robert said, sobbing. "I thought she was dead." For a long time after that, he wasn't quite himself.

But Rita saw him when she could. Margaret caught brief glimpses of her as she came to take him away and then to bring him back, a flurry of thick dark hair and startled eyes, And then one day Robert came back from a day with Rita and said, "My mom told me I have only one Mom." And so Margaret's brief exalted title was put away.

Margaret would like to tell Rita she wishes she hadn't said that to Robert. Rita has them both; it doesn't seem fair. When it became clear that Peter could not keep on loving Margaret, he told her that he'd spent all his love on Rita. She asked him this, knowing he had no answer: "Is love something you can give only once, spent like pennies, only so much and then it's gone?"

She doesn't think she can learn from her mistakes any longer. Nothing quite makes sense. Nothing tells her why the price is so high for these mistakes. She thought that love was something you got more of, the more of it you did. But that was merely an idea. There is a silence in the prairie grasses when the wind stops. The sky comes down flat and very wide. She does not know which direction is better than another. Without the mountains to tell her, "Here is West," she doesn't know which way to turn.

Rita touches her arm. "Look, there's a hawk." Margaret squints in the direction she is pointing and sees, yes, a shape on the fence across the field. Margaret is pleased that Rita would be a person who notices hawks. They've walked along this paved trail in silence, and now Rita has given her this.

They come to a log sanded smooth to serve as a bench. The mountain trails Margaret hiked did not have benches. She suggests they sit, for she thinks that until they're face to face they won't talk, though she has no idea what they might talk about. She'd like to ask her some questions: "How can you not see more of Robert? Why do they both love you so much when you've given so little?" And she would like to ask her, ask anyone: "What is wrong with me?"

Rita's legs are long, and she sprawls on the bench as if she belongs here, as if she belongs wherever she is. Margaret thinks she might be prettier than Rita. But what Rita has is magnetism. Maybe it's her eyes set too wide apart, making her look like a spirited animal that can see around itself for danger.

Margaret thinks Rita ought to ask her about Robert, but Rita seems oddly uninterested in why she called to see her, seems content simply to be with her. The wind has come up again and whips the dark hair around her face. She doesn't bother to brush it back. Margaret's hair is very fine and irritates her in the wind. She can't help it, she keeps pushing her hair off her face with her hand, though she'd rather not seem so nervous. "What did you say your husband does?" Margaret asks finally.

"I didn't." Rita turns to look at her squarely. "He drinks."

Margaret cannot think how to reply.

"He drinks. I drink. We drink together. Sometimes we drink apart."

"I see."

"No. You don't. Sometimes we don't drink. That, too." Rita is smiling a little as if she might enjoy a reaction.

Margaret won't give her that. "My father drank," she says. She will insist on some kinship with her. Rita wants them to be separate, but Margaret has had enough of separation.

Rita curls up her fingers, studies her nails. The cuticles are ragged and red. Margaret notes this with relief and thinks,

"Somewhere she suffers."

"My father died from drinking," Margaret says, matching Rita's sufferings with one of her own. But she is sorry immediately. Now she has seemed to be preaching, and Peter has told her that she preaches insufferably. But what it was, as with what she just said to Rita, was a plea: "Please be interested in what we have in common." Is that, she wonders, a wrong thing to want?

Rita stands up. The knobby weed-grasses knock against each other in the wind. These weeds spend themselves lavishly—dropping seeds, touching each other, nodding and bowing in hectic communal agreement on a single and absolute imperative: grow.

Rita looks tall and very strong as she stands over Margaret. Rita reaches her hands down to raise Margaret up and says, "Come home with me. Meet Steven. Maybe a drink."

Margaret is pleased but a little bit afraid.

Robert sat next to his father clutching the mountain sketch that he'd carefully rolled up and fastened with a rubber band. Margaret wished he didn't plan to give it to his mother and hoped her wish didn't show. He was pale and worried because Rita had just called to say she would be a little late. He knew what late meant. Peter and Margaret were braced for this, but nothing could ever quite prepare them for the child's loss, a loss he seemed fated to experience again and again.

Eventually Robert moved out to the front porch to wait for Rita. Peter glanced up from the newspaper he was reading. He and Margaret looked at each other, sighed and shook their heads.

"I just hate what she does to him," Peter said.

"I do too," she said. She paused, wanting to choose the right words. "I worry that he thinks there's something wrong with him. We keep saying only nice things about her, and so maybe he's forced to conclude it's his fault she keeps standing him up."

Peter laid down the paper, pulled off his glasses. He had thick drooping brows that made his eyes look sad and sincere like a clown's. His mother sent him away right after he was born. Margaret wondered if a person ever recovered from something like that. She wanted to trace those eyebrows with her fingers, but something about him told her she shouldn't. It was as if he didn't want her to love him. She'd become shy, examining beforehand everything she did and said. It seemed clear that if only she could let him alone, he'd want to move toward her. But in this she had failed, for she could never let him alone enough. "What do you suggest I do?" he said. "I can't say bad things about his own mother!"

"Not bad things. But maybe explain a little about her drinking, that some people have a problem and it doesn't mean they don't care, they just can't help it?" She was awash in uncertainty. She would be blamed if this were a bad idea, but she didn't know how to keep from having ideas. The fabric of lies they'd spun around Rita had them caught each in their little pocket of pain, hung there separate and unable to cry out. She could not allow it. And so she kept offering her ideas and her feelings. She would speak out, take the blame. It was foolish, she knew. But what else could she do? It seemed as imperative as the need to dive into a pool when someone is drowning.

The apartment smells of stale beer and incense. Everywhere are dried weeds. They seem not to be arranged, but spray out abundantly from assorted jars and vases as if to assert a power greater than order. There are matted photos on the walls, mostly of Rita. The furniture is mismatched and old, but the sofa has quality velvet fabric, worn as it is, and the arms of it are curled around solid oak. On that sofa sits a man who looks much younger than Rita. He has a thick shock of black hair and stunning blue eyes, put in, as the Irish say, with a sooty finger. He isn't drinking at all, but has a box on his lap and is holding a slide up to the light. A camera is slung around his neck.

He rises, kisses Rita on the forehead, bows in Margaret's direction, gives her a dazzling smile. She brushes her hair off her face, hooks it behind an ear, unhooks it. Rita stares at her, smiling, her hands on her hips. Margaret realizes that the woman has a sense of the absurd, that she enjoys the oddness of this as much as she herself might if she weren't feeling at a disadvantage.

Rita moves toward the kitchen. "Drink? All I have is bourbon or beer."

Margaret rarely drinks, but she says, "A little bourbon with water, please." Steven leads her to an overstuffed chair draped with a Madras bedspread. Rita hands her the drink, gives Steven a can of beer, sits down next to him with a mug of coffee. She nods to the mug deprecatingly and says, "I'm off the stuff for a while." They sit there silently, sipping their drinks. From time to time, Steven holds another slide to the light. Rita picks up Margaret's glass, refills it. They sip some more.

Steven asks Rita to look at a slide. She squints into the light and says, "That's good." She hands it back and says, "You ought to do her." Then she leans toward Margaret, her hair falling over one eye. "The most wonderful moment of my life," Rita says, "was when I gave birth to Robert."

The bourbon has seeped treacherously into a place somewhere behind Margaret's solar plexus and she begins, absurdly, to laugh.

It is that wonderful sort of laughter that begins with great gulps of air—bellows fanning the spark, a donkey winding up for a bray, a diver getting ready for the long one. Take your pick; it doesn't matter, for this is out of her control. It is almost sexual, the way the breaths come from the very bottom of herself, this insistent cadence stronger and older than the word, "Yes!" Clown eyes. Mistakes. Muh-muh-muh. Mountains. It doesn't matter which. There are no levels of difficulty for what has been lost, no levels of logic to contain this convergence of nonsense and utter certainty.

Being taken over like this. It has been a long time for Margaret. Peter was a brilliant and beautiful man. So she never understood why, but he pressed down on the deep shafts of air until they became the shallow breaths you take when you're always waiting. Took this body and made it unsure, self-conscious, subject to doubt. How was this done? Surely she consented. When those sad eyes began refusing to meet hers, when he made love without kissing, she tried to talk to him about it. But in the end, she thought, "Better than nothing." Not without grief. She missed her body. She missed the airy and wild bewilderment of losing herself in him. But then, she no longer had herself to lose, for she'd let him capture her.

So this is her body taking herself back. It clutches into itself like a hand greedy for what it has missed and squeezes until she is flowing out so many tears she thinks there is a river inside. She cannot care that she must sound completely crazy. She can only accept this relief, this peculiar joy, which is almost like singing, or like her mother as she came to her once in a dream.

Rita is standing behind her; her hands stroke her hair. She is saying something. What she's saying is, "He didn't love me either."

"Who didn't?"

She laughs gently. "I don't mean Robert. Robert loves both of us." She rests her hands on Margaret's shoulders, is silent a moment, and then says, "Let's take him."

Margaret shakes her head to clear it, wipes her eyes with the back of her hand.

"You can stay with us. We'll raise him together."

Margaret stands up, turns to face her. Rita's eyes are clear and full of sober intelligence. Margaret looks into those eyes as if they could tell her that such a thing could happen and that she's allowed to listen to this sudden surge of joy. She looks around the room. It has color, a kind of warmth, and Steven, with his camera and tidy boxes of slides, looks like a man who cares about things. But she cannot think clearly, and she speaks without thinking, "Why now? What about all those times you didn't come for him?"

Rita backs away from her, pushing at the air between them with her palms. Steven walks up to stand beside her, slips an arm around her waist. She shakes him off, moves sideways. Her eyes have changed. "Don't preach to me about Robert. Peter took Robert away from me. He took him from the doctor, held him first. I had to beg him for my baby. And then, when I finally got to hold him, somehow it was too late."

Steven has lifted the camera and is shooting her. She spins on her toes as if she's dancing. She speaks in a kind of chant: "I never understood what happened. I couldn't find the bond."

Steven darts from one side of her to the other, clicking the shutter, whirling as she whirls, avoiding the sweep of her arms. She cups one of her breasts and lifts it outward. Now she shouts: "Not even my milk! He wouldn't give us even that!" The camera clicks. Another good one. Steven is panting a little. He turns and aims the camera at Margaret.

"No," she says, and raises her palm to the lens. It is very important that he not do this. She whirls away from them and goes into the kitchen, finds a paper towel, blows her nose. The drying tears on her face feel stiff. She stays in the kitchen a while to compose and remove herself.

The wedding pictures. She noticed at the time and commented to Peter: "Robert is in the middle every time." And then, "It is always Robert you are touching, never me, your bride." A mistake. Peter said, "You are a petty woman. Of a mere child you stoop to be jealous."

"He is like me," he said. "He is my life."

Yes. Well.

She was happy when he called her Mom, and she told this to Peter. Another mistake. She knows this much now, though she doesn't know if she'll decide to accept all of what Rita has said. Rita could have resisted, fought, could have done what Margaret was not able to do either.

Other things are wrong with her, but Margaret thinks she knows the main thing: she was there. In some states the police ticket you for an accident when it was clearly not your fault. The reason they give is, "Being there." Peter doesn't want Robert to have a mother, she thinks, even if he could find one who doesn't make mistakes. The two of them, swimming just fine, are safe from the harm that mothers can do.

Margaret returns to the living room. Rita and Steven are kissing, something more. His hands are cupped over her buttocks and she is writhing and pushing her long legs against his. A vase of dried weeds has been knocked over, and little seeds are scattered on the bare floor.

Margaret picks up her coat, walks to the door. Steven sees her, backs away from Rita, lifts up his camera and cocks the film. She rushes out the door before he can capture her.

Robert seemed stricken when Margaret and Peter told him they were splitting up, but he looked cheerful enough the last time she saw him. He'd begun to draw birds, and he showed Margaret a page of his birds—birds flying, birds preening, birds singing, some of them sparrows, one that might have been an eagle. He'd finally used crosshatching, which she'd shown him a few months before, when he wasn't quite ready. He hugged her for a long time, said, "I wish you weren't leaving." She hugged him back, kissed the top of his head, said, "Me, too."

Peter did not get up from the sofa when she left for that last time. She's not sure why, but that bothers her most of all. Surely in those seven years there was something to be honored, something worthy of the brief ceremony of rising and saying good-bye.

The winds join forces and come at her with clubs and boots, making her stagger and run to the car. She is thinking maybe Chicago, where a few relatives live who might put her up while she looks for work. Drew and Susan, her dearest friends, have moved only a few hundred miles south of there, and she suspects she'll be needing them.

She tells herself she will send a postcard to Robert from the first place she stops. Now and then she'll send little gifts, art things, maybe that new kind of clay you can fire in an ordinary oven. She'd always meant to do clay with him. Maybe Peter will let him visit her once she's settled. He would never send him here to stay with Rita, which she thinks is probably wise. She hopes Peter realizes, that despite her own mistakes, there's nothing too much wrong with her, nothing like that.

She pauses a moment to remember which way north is, then heads for the freeway. She'll head up to I-70, then go east, crossing the arc of the sun, against the movement of light. She feels oddly ashamed of this, as if she's disobeying a fundamental law. The car rocks in the wind and she knows this is going to be tiring, but she'll go as far north as she can before she stops to sleep. She is not sure if Chicago is a good idea, but it's a place to start. There's a cousin she might stay with for a while until she gets her bearings. Here, two rivers have met and converged. The wind from Mexico and the wind from the Arctic slap across each other like hands signaling the end of something. Even so, these winds will keep pushing at the grass and the sky as if to bring them together, too.

The Great Barrier Reef

The man Joy long-ago loved had begged her to flee to Canada with him, but it made no sense to her, his passion against war when God and family and everyone else saw war as a righteous thing. So Joy lived on with her parents and her younger sister Grace for a few years. Then Grace married Alfred and moved into town, and, not long after, their parents died and left Joy the farm, which she promptly sold. This was how she was able to buy a little house, dig out a garden, take up acrylic landscape painting, and glide through the years without complaint. Joy's code was this: that she be happy and see every rising moment in a positive light.

Her house was on the edge of town. It faced a flat expanse of farmland planted in orderly rows of corn. Each morning Joy stood at her doorway to watch the sun come up, or, if it was overcast, which it often was, to watch the pale band of light spread like enamel across the horizon. Flocks of dark birds twisted and swooped over the corn into a kaleidoscope of shapes: a diamond, a triangle, a circle, a rollover twist in perfect formation, down to become flat, like a hand blessing the tips of the corn, or like a platter of birds serving up the sky of the day.

On this particular day, she'd planned an afternoon of bedding the annuals; she was especially looking forward to arranging the cockscombs and the border of petunias. But it was raining. Because she made it a point never to dwell on the negative, she laughed, tilted her head into the rain and said, "Oh, yes. Now I have time to paint." And paint she did, another landscape, awash in lavender and peach, overlaid here and there with tiny black vees to represent the birds. For two hours exactly she perched on a stool at her easel and painted.

While she did this, she performed her affirmations, saying aloud, as she did every unfailing day, good things about herself: "I am an artist. I am creative. I am a child of God." She'd read about affirmations in a book her mother—who was really quite up-to-date—gave her not long before she died. Next to God, certain books were to be believed in. If you did what they said, you'd be as right as the gleam on a raindrop, you'd have things to be thankful for, everything to look forward to. On this day in particular, she felt a sense of possibility, of, even, excitement. Something was going to happen, she knew it, to touch her in a new way. Her eyes went soft into the colors of her landscape

Peach was her favorite, the queen of colors: babyskin, Sweet William, the first breath of sunrise, the dabs of light on the undersides of leaves, or so she had decided. Peach. You could cup one in your hand and hold it to your cheek and think it pressed itself to you of its own accord, a thing alive. And then, you ate it, eager for the best part at the end: the tangy shreds clinging to the pit, which you sucked, if no one was around, until your lips were sore.

Alfred and her sister Grace were coming to dinner tonight, and perhaps this had something to do with her mood of anticipation. Alfred loved his peaches and tonight she was serving peaches with whipped cream (the real kind) and shortcake. Grace, well, it didn't matter, for she was ill and loved hardly anything at all, nor did she have an ounce of gratitude for having a husband like Alfred. Give him a bowl of sliced fresh peaches, a little half-and-half, offer him a smile, a nod, and the man was happy. What she wouldn't give! Ah well, no use in dwelling on that.

Last year, when Grace's illness had received its terrible name, Joy knelt down before her sister, took the hollow-boned hands into her own, and said, "Just repeat after me, 'I am full of life.'"

"But I am not full of life," Grace said.

And Joy rose up, brushed off her knees, her duty done. She tried again another day, and yet again. Once, maybe it was last month, Grace had squeezed back with her hands and said, "Joy, please let me talk about what's happening to me."

This caused the colors surrounding Joy to tear a little, like a chiffon scarf caught on a nail, and through the jagged hole she could see darkness and cruelty. And so she said to Grace, "What is happening to you is what you create."

"It isn't my fault, what's happening to me," Grace had said.

"But it is your fault," Joy had thought. After that, she had nothing left to try.

Joy washed off her brushes and poured out the tin of paint water, wishing the colors wouldn't turn muddy and dark in the water. It was like pouring out a burnt pot, and she'd had the thought more than once that the water was more the product of her labor than was her painting. And so to affirm her paintings she had her favorite ones framed and hung them on a wall in the living room; she'd even had the sofa re-upholstered to match the tones of her art.

She checked to make sure the lamb chops were thawed, prepared a salad, tidied the place, took a shower, dressed in soft colors and softened the ends of her graying hair with a curling iron. "I am a fine-looking woman," she told her reflection in the bathroom mirror, leaning back a little to take in more of her youthful slenderness. Then she moved closer to the lean face that was herself. For one terrible moment she thought she saw tiny lines threading up from her lip like gathered silk, the most grotesque sort of wrinkles, not at all like the friendly crinkles around her eyes. Her breath caught, clamping down against a sudden dark dread. Then she shook herself, smiled, and the new wrinkles disappeared. "Stop that," she said. "You are an ageless child of God."

They arrived promptly at six, Grace tottering on Alfred's strong arm. Alfred let go of his wife for a moment to shake the rain from the umbrella. A button on his shirt was broken in half; the skin under his nice eyes was shadowed; he didn't look like a man who was loved. Grace clutched at the crocheted afghan wrapped around her shoulders. The woman wasn't even out of her forties yet, and here she was wearing an old-lady afghan, her face pinched up like a prune, ludicrous in contrast to the curly wig she wore now. Joy wanted to feel some charity for her sister, tried to summon up sympathy for her grave illness, but she couldn't, because it came down to one thing: Grace did not think positively. She'd been the one in the family to bring up unpleasant things. Back then you could ignore her. These days there was a trembling anger to her; she was a knapped flint, everything smooth and round cleaved away and all you had left was that terrible edge.

And so it was good when Grace was silent. Alfred tore into the lamb chops; grease accumulated on his chin. More than once he exclaimed, "What a pleasure! What a delight! You are too good to us!" Joy longed to reach out with her napkin to wipe away the grease. He needed taking care of.

Grace ate very little; she remained blessedly silent for most of the main course, but just as Joy was about to clear the plates, Grace said, "They've left a hole in my head where they took out some bone. They want to go back in and fill it up with coral."

Joy was taken by surprise, and she interrupted Alfred, who was on the verge of silencing his wife. "Coral?" she said.

Grace laughed a little. "Yes, coral. The Great Barrier Reef; they want to put a piece of it my head."

"Whatever for?" Joy leaned towards her, interested despite her resolve to steer her sister away from these discussions.

"It's supposed to bond with the bone, grow and fill in the gaps." She laid down her fork and smiled. "It would be rather wonderful to have a piece of the ocean in my head. I'd be part of something beautiful and grand. Imagine!"

Joy didn't know what to say to that. She thought of pictures she'd seen of beaches where the water curved along the shore in brilliant blue petals like enormous flowers. She thought of barracuda, electric eels, muscular pearl divers with knives in their teeth. And suddenly she felt an overwhelming envy for her sister. She envied her and envied everyone who'd gone to new places and seen shocking, beautiful things.

Then Grace screwed up her face into its normal prune-look. "But what's the point? They couldn't get it all. The gaps will fill up soon enough."

Joy was sorry she'd encouraged her sister to speak. She cleared the plates and led them into the living room. Grace gathered her afghan around herself, hugging it tightly as if she were cold, and curled up on the sofa. Joy went to the kitchen to make the coffee and shortcake.

Alfred came into the kitchen just as Joy had finished whipping up the cream. His eyes were bright and he dabbed around his mouth with a napkin. Then he stepped up close to her. Joy thought he was going to reach for the spoon, ask if he could help. She smelled spice and flowers, heard his breath draw in like someone about to dive, saw his foot pivot and lurch. In a sudden almost painful rush, with a gasp and a sorrowful moan, he put his arms around her, held on, pressed tighter.

"I've wanted to do this for so long!" he whispered.

Joy bit at her lower lip, first to keep from wincing, then to keep from smiling. She allowed herself the pressure of his chest against hers, the fine hurtful clench of his arms, the sense that she was swooping into the sea like a great bird. She allowed this, and then she pulled in her stomach and breathed in everything she knew was right, for this was the only way to live as a child of God. She pushed him away, raised her flat palms in front of her face as if to inscribe a wall of righteousness through which no waters, no salt, no electric currents must flow, and she said, because she must, "Shame on you. Shame."

Joy kept her eyes downcast as she set the peaches and cream and coffee on the tray, but she could feel Alfred's eyes burning and begging, and she allowed herself to think, "So this is what was meant to happen."

The two of them came out to Grace, who clung to the fraying edges of her afghan with bony hands. She smiled up at them a crooked little smile, a smile which had once been wistful, gamin-like. Now the smile was distorted from nerve damage. She didn't raise a hand against her illness, Joy remembered, wouldn't even consider doing the affirmations she'd tried to teach her.

Alfred and Joy sat down across from each other; Grace was a little off to the side on the pastel sofa. In the middle was a low table on which the tray of coffee and dessert had been placed. Alfred smiled full on Joy. The two of them licked the whipped cream on their lips, sucked the peach slices into their mouths, and allowed crumbs to dribble from their forks, never taking their eyes off one another. The subtlety of this excited Joy.

Grace pushed her fork at her shortcake for a while, then gave up the effort and sat back, snuggled into the sofa, and closed her eyes. Alfred's eyes never moved from Joy's face, and he said nothing, not even to praise the peaches. The silence seemed eloquent with promises, as if some vow, some proposal, even, were being made. Joy couldn't help it. She was happy. With a surge of generosity, she reached over and touched Grace's knee, wanting to include her in this happiness.

Grace snapped open her eyes, blinked, and apologized for dozing. Then she tilted her head toward the wall of Joy's paintings and said, her lips pursed in that unbecoming way, "Your paintings are too pretty, my dear. Why won't you let them do something interesting?"

Joy snatched her hand away from her sister's knee. She turned to Alfred, expecting his support, for he had once had said hers was serious art indeed. But he smiled and winked at her, which was not to the point of the moment at all. His smile seemed to say that what flowed between them like a river was murky and not very clean. She was confused, her feelings clashing and mixing and canceling out. "I have failed," came the one clear thought, "to matter to anyone."

She stood up quickly and began picking up the coffee cups and the dirty plates, piled them on the tray. She wanted to go outside and weed her garden.

"I need to talk about dying," Grace said.

"For cry-eye, Grace," said Alfred.

Joy knelt down to some crumbs on the carpet and brushed at them with her hand.

"Both of you are afraid," Grace said. "I'm the one who should be afraid." Her eyes darted back and forth between the two of them, as if she were following a tennis match.

Alfred sighed and said, "Grace, you're tired, let's go home."

"Yes, I'm tired." Grace's eyes stopped moving and fixed themselves at something she'd just seen in her thoughts. "What's the matter with you two? Are you ashamed?

Alfred hurried Grace to the door, as much as she could be hurried with her arms tangled in the afghan and her legs unsteady, her eyes not as focused as they used to be. He picked up the umbrella and shook it out sharply, and said in a forced jovial voice, "I'm sorry, Joy, to eat and run, but Grace has to get her beauty sleep, you know." And he winked again at Joy, and she turned her face away.

"Damn you," said Grace. "This is wrong."

Joy put her fist to her throat and thought, "My God, she knows."

Alfred pulled his wife out into the rain. Joy wanted to run after, to tear at him and say, "Look what you've done! She's my sister!"

Grace grabbed hold of the door frame, leaned back into the house, and called out, "Dying isn't anything to be ashamed of! You don't have to be ashamed of me!"

The next day Joy went out into the rain and bought a bushel of overripe peaches from the truck farmer down the road. She placed the peaches on her kitchen floor in neat rows and admired them as if she'd planted them and they'd come up like obedient stalks of corn. She walked among the peaches and wondered what she'd done, wondered if anything existed now to make things right. She could think of nothing, and with this understanding came rage, electric and white, like the belly of a seabird.

Joy put her rain boots back on, and stamped. She stamped and danced and stamped, until the peaches spread into a stippled pool of dark slime. Then she took off her boots and her coat, and lay belly down on the floor, kicked and flailed her arms and swam into the crushed fruit. She rolled and arched her body, thrust her wing bones against the pits. For the first time in years, she thought of the long-ago man who had begged her to go to Canada with him, the way his eyes closed like last moons when she said, "I'll never leave this place." She remembered and cried aloud the thing she would never say again: "I am a person incapable of love."

Finally she quieted and lay there, staring at the thing she had done. The squashed peaches oozed through her fingers like the mud in her garden. "What can grow from this?" she wondered and nearly despaired again, but only for a moment, for it was time, she knew, to take herself in hand. She cupped the shreds and slime into her hands, heaped them onto old newspapers, bundled them up, thrust them into a black plastic leaf bag. The pits she tossed into a bucket, thinking she'd plant a few in along the fence line. It occurred to her that she ought to shower and dress and fix her hair. But first: paper towels, water, a sponge, a mop. It was a long task and it calmed her, but still the floor was slippery, and seemed as if it might never come clean again.

Oil Exploration

Against the wind and the roar, I scuttle under the whirling blades, climb into the transparent bubble cockpit. The pilot brushes a lock of dark hair out of his eyes, which are an odd fern-like green. He shakes my hand, introduces himself as Adam, asks if this is my first time. A fool, I say yes, and before I can clip my seatbelt, we shoot straight up. Then a sudden bank right, and we're scudding across a blur of sagebrush. The dim horizon tilts, askew with spiky Tetons. A herd of elk scatters under our shadow. A bull moose shakes his rack, stands his ground. We swoop over a sudden cliff. I bite my hand not to scream. The guys sitting behind me cry *yee hah*. George, if he were among them, would try to comfort me, which would undo me completely.

Adam is smiling at my hand-covered mouth, but not unkindly. I think he's letting me feel tested so I can be one of the boys. Finally, we land, and our crew tumbles from the chopper into a high meadow transected by a row of orange surveyor's flags. The meadow is thick with purple flowers, smells of onions and something acrid that makes me think of bears.

We've come to the Line. As Front Crew, our job is to lay thick orange cables along this line and stamp fist-sized plastic spheres called geophones into the ground at exact intervals beside the cables, all of which is finally connected to a seismograph. Dynamite will be detonated, and the resulting vibrations will somehow tell the geologists the dark possibilities of oil.

The Line roams the landscape not as a sensible hiker might, but at the whim of surveyors who carry dowsers or something and divine the presence of oil, say, under a slope of scree unstable as roller bearings, or in the crotch between mountains, where weeds spiral like snakes and spongy grass bleeds into a brimming beaver pond. Then a tumble of boulders pulls our burning legs up and up, and you think it can't get any higher. But the Line bags a peak only to roll like drumbeats over a whole new spread of mountains.

The orange cables and neatly spaced geophones stitch the landscape as if we're binding up some enormous wound in the Earth. Everywhere there's the smell of what I'm sure is bear. I've hiked in mountains often enough, but never someplace that feels so wild, so private, it's like spying on someone who's naked. Sometimes we're in the ponderosa, with reticulated trunks rearing up like giant pythons. Every hour or so Adam comes ratcheting back to lower cables and phones on the longline. Because of the threat of snagging the longline on the trees, the crew says Adam's work is as dangerous as was his stint in Vietnam.

I'm the first woman. There's another, Laurie, hired on the second day. She has double eyelashes, a genetic rarity I thought bestowed only on the likes of Elizabeth Taylor. I find myself staring, try not to let it show. She doesn't talk much, carries a stash, shares it with the crew. This is wise: the only reason we two are here is Affirmative Action. The crew foreman barks spasmodically every fifteen minutes or so something like: "Cunts on the line! I hate! I hate!" He has a flat round face like a pie, and eyes stuck in as if by harried thumbs, utterly without expression.. But I can see he's warming up to Laurie's pocketful of hash. The crew's mania for drugs is a complication, because George and I swore off a couple years ago.

As a policy, the company separates husband and wife, so George is a few miles behind on the Dynamite Crew. George and I sleep in my old blue Civic because the Camp bunkhouse is filthy. I don't mind. I've got the best kind of tiredness. It's cozy and complete to curl on the narrow reclining seat and hug a pillow. But George is horny. Because of this he punched his fist into the windshield, so now it's cracked.

No shower for weeks, it's finally our two days off, so George and I head for a motel, slather suds over each other like newlyweds. As soon as we hit the squeaky double bed, we're dead asleep. The next morning George goes out with his fat paycheck and trades my sweet little Civic with its cracked windshield for a rattly pickup with a camper shell, buys a lumpy old mattress, throws it in the back. Driving back to the camp, he hums Red River Valley, sneaks sideways amber looks, and I resolve to make him happy.

Sometimes our crew ends a day on a peak and the chopper can't land, has to hover several feet off the ground. We have to reach for the skids, wrestle our way up into the chopper. It's not something I ever thought I could do. I love the new steel of my body and Adam's approving smile. I love the way his dark hair keeps falling over his ferny eyes, and the easy way he talks. He tells me about Vietnam, how one time he landed in a jungle clearing amidst a terrible crossfire and rescued some buddies. He says it was a miracle, so his life since then is a temporary gift he's enjoying for all he can. He says we didn't belong in Vietnam, wishes he'd run to Canada.

I love it now when he does wild things with the chopper. Sometimes he auto-rotates a landing. About fifty feet up he shuts off the engine, and slowly we turn, descending a soundless winding staircase. It's a magical feat that silences everyone, even the foreman. Laurie never talks, keeps her eyes shuttered by those astonishing lashes, and the men like her all the more.

George tells me about a new woman on the Dynamite Crew who first thing out of the chopper takes off her shirt. She doesn't wear a bra, and she has, George says, the most perfect breasts he's ever seen. He tells me this because he's angry. George is an open-hearted, glowing sort of man, with amber eyes and wild hair that matches. I don't know why I can't. There's the camper shell now, a mattress to lie on together, and still I can't, as if these mountains have come between us and the possibility of love. I lie awake and think of the way Adam plays the scales of the wind like a horn.

George tells me that Adam is on coke and acid and also speed, says everyone is. I wonder why anyone would need drugs in such a beautiful place, would even consider such a thing when even a small mistake could mean death. George says that's why they use—can't face the beauty, or the danger, straight on. I look at him hard, surprised at his wisdom, wonder if the job is changing him, too. He tells me they fired the perfect-breasted girl because when they shot off the dynamite she screamed and writhed on the ground. The noise does that to some people. I wonder what it does to the bears. I try to talk to him about the bears and the beaver dams and how I think we shouldn't be here. He laughs, says I should think instead about all the money we're making so he can finish college and start to catch up to me. I can't convince him that Ph.D.s are a dime a dozen, but a great carpenter—which he is—belongs to an endangered species we must nurture and protect.

This time the nimble surveyors have taken the Line over a steep granite outcropping that should be climbed with ropes. At camp around a small fire are endless discussions about who should do this climb to lay out the cables and phones, detonate the charges, how it can be done, which sort of ropes, caribiners, chocks, slings, and so on must be supplied. George and I have rock climbing experience—vouched for by Ian, who got us this job, though he's now somewhere in California—so we're to join this operation, which has taken on the proportions of an Everest expedition. The Front Line foreman, Pie, will go. Laurie, too. It turns out she's a ski patroller from Jackson Hole; an amazing array of outdoor skills come to light once they draw her out. She's so modest I feel gauche for ever having said a word about myself.

The granite juts up in a series of narrow arcs, as if wheels of rock had tried to roll upwards and gotten stuck halfway inside the mountain. Little firs angle out in the cracks; swatches of heavy grass claw at a few lopsided ledges. Here and there are the orange surveyor's flags, placed not logically for the easiest climb, of course, but according to the mysterious divinings of the right kind of shale swallowed deep in the belly of this massif. The granite is rough-textured, nubbed with heavy crystals and pocked inward or cracked at generous intervals. Probably a 5.8 at the hardest spots, which means maybe one or two technical moves, nothing acrobatic.

Pie, as I call him, leads the first pitch, and Laurie follows, the heavy cable slung crossways over her shoulders. An easy set of bucket holds so far, but you have to admire the flow of her moves under all that weight. I am belayed last, and every few feet I plant a geophone—somewhere, anywhere: in a nest of soil where two thighs of granite converge, behind the twisted roots of a tree, in an unpromising crack. It's impossible to do this right. For certain, the phones will fall out, most of them. As I haul myself over the top of the pitch, Pie gives me a goofy grin and waves a joint. Nothing connects him to the rock. He has belayed me without having tied himself in. If I'd fallen, I'd most likely have pulled him off the rock—to land on top of me, God forbid. Laurie stands there, oblivious, maybe stoned herself.

I can't help it, I yank on the back of his harness, which should have been anchored, and yell, "You idiot! Don't you know the first thing?" Laurie gives me a startled look, then hides behind her astonishing lashes, gets busy fastening in the cable, organizing her knots. She does seem to understand well enough to insist on leading the next, and final pitch—me as her belay from below, and herself as belay from up above—with Pie coming last to plant the strand of useless geophones.

This last pitch has some interesting sections: a layback on a flake of granite, where you have to pull against your hands and push with your feet, turning yourself into a living cam of sorts; and a jam crack, where you slice in your hand flat, then fist it, pull yourself up with that fist., and then the next flat hand, and fist, and so on. With your feet, you twist in the ball of your foot sideways, then ease it whatever way will give you purchase to rise. It's hard on the knuckles, hell on incipient bunions, but a huge rush, because you've done something that doesn't intuitively seem possible—and done it unrolling a fat orange cable all the while.

Pie has a tough time coordinating the climb and trying to plant the phones. There aren't many little pockets of soil in this section: can't jam metal spikes into solid rock. I don't know why the surveyors thought of crossing here, where nothing can possibly jiggle that nervous little needle on the seismograph, that MRI of the mountains. Pie yells his head off during the jam crack, takes a fall on the flake, but Laurie catches him smartly. Anchored she is. I'll give her that.

We're all three finally at the top, untying, coiling ropes, which snag on bony claws of greasewood and clumps of sagebrush; the back of this outcrop is a gentle slope washing us into high desert. This sudden new landscape is a shock after so much alpine, and we stumble around some and reel away from each other as if we've been thrown out of some late-night booze joint.

Pie starts yelling and flailing his pack at something on the other side of a rock. "Rattlesnake!" he cries. "Lousy dirty rotten snake!" He is out of control, crazy. Laurie runs to him, grabs his arm, yanks him backward, cries, "You'll get bitten!" I can't help it, inch over to see. The snake is a large sand-colored diamondback, so beautiful I almost forget to be afraid. He is the wiser one, uncoils, flows like spring-water into a tangle of sage and broken-up granite and vanishes.

Pie finally settles down, smokes, falls asleep. We have the rest of the day to relax on top of the granite until Adam comes for us.

George tells me they didn't even bother setting off any charges on that face, though he and a few others still got to climb and remove the cables and phones. It was a pointless, expensive day for the company; a delightful diversion for some of the crew; a lucky escape for the snake. George and I laugh at the foolishness of others, congratulate our own good sense, our day of fun. I smell cordite and purple onions in his hair. I love it when George and I do nothing but hug and play.

We're like children together at our best. Maybe that's why. When he tries to be a man, he sets out to cipher me, decode me, open and close me, all translated and set in hard type. I can't let him do this. Then comes his imploring love, a monster I've created by my own hand that pushes him away, makes him need and need and need. I'm going to have to let him go. It isn't fair. This isn't what he bargained for. I seem not to be a proper woman, as if something in my upbringing didn't break me in correctly. I'm not accepted even by the lights of a ragtag seismic crew. Ian was the only man who saw me as all right just as I was, maybe even wonderful. But he moved away, sent us two postcards: one from Alaska saying he'd done McKinley; then much later, from Berkeley saying he was going to visit his brother and take a little rest from all that climbing. I'd never known he had a brother, never knew of him to take a rest. But then, Ian isn't someone you can set in stone.

Now we wear orange vests issued by the company. It's hunting season; Wyoming hunters will shoot at anything, they say, even choppers. Today was unseasonably hot, and we're out of water and done with our cables. Adam finally comes, but he says only two can board this trip because he has to pick up a couple of head honchos who've been slumming it with the dynamite crew. I'm in no hurry to face George's hopeful smile, so it's good that Laurie and Pie hurry aboard. Adam smiles at me, shakes his dark hair, juts up a thumb. The chopper lifts off like a bulbous angel and tips toward a stand of ponderosa on the westward mountain, behind which the sun hangs in orange and purple shreds.

I lie in the nest of some boulders, think about a cold beer, a pillow. Long shadows reach into our silent meadow. I wonder if the elk would come to feed if we weren't here. In the distance, rifle shots, then an explosion too loud for gunfire. The sun seems to coalesce, to burst, then to fall. We all leap up, but no one speaks; we look at each other, look away.

Out of the indigo twilight, another chopper finally comes. On our way back to Camp, the strange pilot tells us nothing. I shiver in the night updraft and know that soon I will feel the enormity of this.

George stands in the anxious crowd at Camp, his hair golden and flaring in the lights of our chopper, the crush of wind. I leap out to him, hold on for dear life, hold on a little longer.

Color Blind

Here we are, two brothers in a hurry, and we're stuck behind a Winnebago that wallows and yaws ten miles below the speed limit. This road is so desolate I can't imagine it leading anywhere good. A sagging line of telephone poles and wires is a hint that civilization is somewhere, but for now it's all sad looking sand, clutches of sagebrush, broom-dry grass, and big wrinkled boulders lying around like dying elephants. In the distance are mesas or bluffs, too far away to count as scenery. I can't see why Alice said we should come this way.

Then again, I've been driving all night, and the sun is barely up, so everything looks kind of flat. Probably, too, there are colors out there I just don't see. Like our father, Ian and I are partially color blind according to the eye test charts. Sometimes green looks like brown, they say. Blue is sort of gray. Alice says this is sad. She says a person needs color in order to feel.

When Ian talked to us a few months back about how he might try Dr. V's clinic in Houston as a last resort, Alice said we ought to drive through Utah on the way. She went on and on about the healing powers of the red rock, especially the arches near Moab. My brother remembers, wants us to go through Moab now. I understand, given the extremity of his need, but spiritual stuff isn't his thing, and I don't even live with Alice anymore.

Ian is asleep, his mouth open because blood has clotted in his sinuses. His head wobbles to the rocking of the car; his skinny knees knob sideways. His hair, which used to be thick and almost black, has begun to grow back, a downy fuzz, a newborn chick. His neck is scrawny like an old man's, but you can still see the long muscles in his arms from all those years of climbing. Any time now, he could slip into something deeper than sleep, and I worry I won't know what to do.

Alice would know—she's a nurse—but I won't be able to call her for advice because last week she flipped her dark hair behind her shoulder, pushed against my chest, said, "Your time's up. Get out." I gathered up my guitar and other things, tumbled out of her house into the morning fog of Half Moon Bay. She has her eye on the biological clock, and if the clock doesn't tick for me, she needs time to find another pair of hands, so to speak.

I called a friend who took me in, and phoned my brother to let him know where I was. Ian said, "Greg, maybe you should marry Alice." I've wondered if he isn't half in love with her himself. It turned out, though, that love wasn't foremost on his mind. What he said next was, "I've gone acute. I had them take a second bone marrow to be sure. I'm almost out of time." Then he laughed like he was making a little joke, said, "So it's time to get serious. I'm ready to try Dr. V's clinic. Can you drive me to Houston?"

I drove my old Volvo wagon up to Berkeley, helped my brother load it with bottled water, Green tea, Chinese herbs, and painkillers. I told him the radio didn't work, but he said he'd mostly sleep anyway. He insisted I leave a message on Alice's answering machine telling her, just in case. "And tell her we're going through Moab," he said, with a little grin, all of which struck me as a bit unkind, given that she'd just kicked me out.

Ian has to travel by car because airplanes are unsafe with their germ-laden cabin-trapped air. He's having a blast crisis, the grand finale of his disease. Immature white blood cells—the blasts—are spewing out of his marrow into his blood like fireworks. He's losing his red cells, his platelets; his T cells are weak. He could live another month or two, another day, another hour. So here we are, in search of a last-minute miracle.

He's a year older than me, forty three. We haven't even gotten started with our lives, neither of us with a family or what anyone would call a career. We did the years of hitching around the country, getting stoned, doing anti-nuke marches, going to college when we felt like it, doing the great outdoors—whatever might keep us from getting swept into the American mainstream. What I think now is that America is one wide muddy river, oozing across the whole world. There's no other side to reach, no swimming out of it.

And so my brother and I are still adrift. I write music, play some, do roadie work for bands, feel sorry for myself because I don't have a family, but then I have to be honest and look at the fact that I'm afraid to get married. Ian used to guide mountain climbers, but then he started to say he felt tired, that maybe it was time to quit climbing and get a life. He said he was ready to find a smart, strong woman, have a child: a little girl he saw as if she was already born, with chestnut hair and hazel eyes like mine. He was always good about saving money, which is how he can afford to try Dr. V.

The last few years he's lived in a group house in Berkeley with a bunch of other climbers. He likes the idea of creating something different than a family, where people live together based on a shared passion, like climbing, not out of romantic or biological obligation. I can see why he leans that way. In our original family, love and obligation turned in on itself like blood gone bad, a sad mix of alcohol, blind rage, and dead hopes. I admire how he's tried to rise above that story, but I think his group house is kind of depressing: the piles of used teabags they say they'll use again, but never do, the lists of chores on the fridge, rules about using the TV, shabby mismatched furniture, dim light bulbs, grim-looking women clomping up the stairs in heavy boots, the backpacks and ropes and climbing racks strewn like tinker toys around the living room.

I see certain contradictions, like his pushing the idea of marriage on me—even though he's always called marriage a sick institution—his recent talk of wanting a child. I guess we're both confused.

Ian's climbing family seems to be pulling away from him now that he's terminally ill. No one volunteered to come along to Houston, which would have really helped, and he's told me they seem nervous, almost as if he's already a ghost and they're afraid of him. He says he's all right about this, but I think it's wrong of them, a flaw in the vision. I think mixing people together who all like to do the same thing isn't enough. You need something else, like love. Or maybe it's just luck whatever social glue you try to use.

The Winnebago slows for yet another curve, tilting ungracefully, a foolish contraption only someone without any art at all would design. I despise it, see it as all that's wrong with America: blocky, clumsy, like an overgrown teenager going nowhere, using everything up. Not that Ian and I are much better. This trip is a crazy idea. Even if Dr. V. isn't a quack, it must be too late for any sort of cure. Does my brother know this? Should I help him see?

If Ian would only wake up, we could talk a little—though probably not about that. I want us to argue about politics or economic theories, want not to think about what the world will be like without my brother, what it is already like without Alice. Nothing about the landscape of lonely telephone wires and distant mesas lets me get outside of myself.

Alice lived in Moab with her first husband, a river rat who ran float trips and couldn't keep his hands off those tan-legged spray-soaked clients. She left him, moved to the California coast where she met me, but Moab is where she wishes she could still live. She's joined a church, which says a lot about how desperate she is. Though she tries to act cheerful, sometimes she's so full of sadness it spews out of her like radioactive dust. Even so, her eyes make me feel like she really sees me; her hugs bring me home to a place I forgot I ever lived.

But she scares me, and that makes her mad. It's not just the baby thing. She says I don't listen to her feelings. What does it mean to listen to feelings? It's like saying you should be able to see the air. I can listen to music and understand the counterpoint, hear the key changes, anticipate progressions. I can play along with anyone on my guitar, improvise, be a part of someone else's music. But Alice's feelings make sounds I can't follow—loud sounds, like crying or shouting—and the best I manage is what I feel in return, which is mostly confusion, a little fear, a lot of being pissed off. There seems to be no way to join any of this to what she's feeling, whatever that might be. How do men and women ever learn to get along?

For my brother, I have feelings, but I can't think how to show them. He hates for anyone to fuss over him. While he was visiting me,

I drove him to the doctor because he'd been having night sweats and chest pain. When he finally came back into the waiting room, he reeled into a chair.

He stared up at me like a puzzled little kid, said, "I've got leukemia."

I ran over to him, put my hand on his shoulder. He twisted away, said, "Don't make a big deal. Okay? I'm going to lick this thing." So I've tried to be careful.

The very next day he was at the library and online, tracking down the thin possibilities. The only hope held out by conventional medicine was a bone marrow transplant, a slash-and-burn approach that went against his anti-war ideals, which anyway his cheap HMO wouldn't cover. He did relent and have just enough chemo to stave off a dangerous early rise in white blood cells and to lose his hair. That, combined with a macrobiotic diet, Chinese herbs, hypnosis, kept him in remission for six months, during which he researched every alternative, which led him to Dr. V. as his court of last resort.

Dr. V. believes in these peptides that bond with the cancer cells and teach them—at least some of the time—to behave normally, to become useful members of the body instead of childish renegades, which is what leukemia cells are—white cells that run amok, won't grow up.

I think of junior high school and those awful dances when I wanted nothing to do with girls. But then one night I sort of drifted out of my mind like I was walking in my sleep and I asked the prettiest girl to dance. She smelled like new-cut grass. Her hand in mine connected me to myself as if I was a wire they'd forgotten to plug in. Everything changed. Girls became the best thing this life has come up with. I started trying to get along.

With Dr. V's peptides the cancer cells start wanting to hook up to other cells; they go with the music, learn how to dance in the blood. They begin to grow up. It makes wonderful sense, and seems to have worked for other kinds of cancer, but I learned a long time ago that lots of things that make sense don't always work, and there's an amazing amount of resistance in the universe against any sort of bonding.

Alice has a gift for healing—I can tell from her stories about being a nurse—but she's too much like our mother. She feels too much. I

116

wrote songs for Alice, made little speeches about the goodness of life, made her laugh, but it always was, she said, "not the point." That's the hard thing I learned about women after I committed myself to knowing them: they hurt so easily, and this makes me feel I've done something terrible.

The Winnebago turns off at a sign saying Dead Horse Point, and I sigh at the relief of an unobstructed view of road, a little acceleration. The mesas, or whatever they are, have come closer to the road, throwing down aggressive sweeps of rubble. The sand is no longer pale, but reminds me of old blood.

Ian finally wakes up. In the new morning light, the whites of his eyes seem yellow. He coughs, leans forward, his fist to his chest, peers through the windshield. "Nothing worth climbing here," he says.

We're silent awhile. This is one of the great things about Ian. You can have silence and it never feels empty. I'm glad we don't have a radio to distract us from this good silence. Now that he's back with me, I no longer feel pressed to talk, and the horrible Winnebago is gone. We can stretch our eyes, see the dips and rises, the pale dawn sky smeared with streaky clouds. What I thought were telephone wires has become a militant power line, the kind of electromagnetic field Ian says can give you leukemia.

After a few miles, he says, "I'm ready to get well."

Shouldn't he be at the acceptance stage by now? I'm thinking of a movie I saw where some comedian kept screeching the stages of dying: Denial! Anger! Bargaining! Depression! Acceptance!

"No time like the present," I say, feeling like a coward. I think I sound like our father, who pulled aphorisms out of a hat like a bored magician.

"What do you think Dad would make of this?" he says, as if he's read my mind.

"Make of what?"

"This trip. The cure I'm going to get."

Our father has been dead ten years and we've never been able to say anything about him except, "He was very intelligent," perhaps because he sat night after night, his hand curled around an old-fashioned, silent and sad. All we knew was he did some sort of secret government intelligence work. I feel a wash of tiredness. The sun breaks over a wall of rock, hurts my eyes.

I search for the words I think my brother needs, and I say, "'Great. Go for it.' That's what he'd say."

"I don't think so," Ian says.

"Oh?"

"He'd say, 'That and a dime will get you on the subway.'"

"He would?"

"He didn't believe in anything."

I can't think of what to say. And I wonder what use it is anyway to dredge up a dead father to cheer him on. A raven swoops onto the road, and I swerve.

"I believe in you," I say.

"Not really. You're scared to death."

"Well, of course I'm a little worried," I say. Ian's eyes are closed again.

My brother and I shared a room for almost eighteen years. He kept his side neat. Mine was never right, cluttered with records and sheets of music, and clothes I could never make myself hang up. When he slept, he sometimes mumbled and cried out, mewed like a kitten. But in the daytime he was the quiet one. I had a tendency to interrupt him when he was about to speak, and I feel really bad, remembering this. I was a clown person, always needing to make people notice me. Ian, he'd get sort of gathered up, his face tight with the fullness of some new idea, but then he'd stop, let me steal the show. What was it he wanted to say?

This road goes on and on. It rises, falls, turns, straightens. I'm so tired of roads. I feel a surge of anger at Alice. She was so friendly to Ian, sometimes I wondered if she was trying to belong to us both.

"There's red rock ahead." It's my brother, awake after all.

"How can you tell?" I can't see any red, but maybe his color blindness isn't exactly like mine.

"Alice told me," he says. "She told me she has her church friends praying for me."

I think how stupid of her. Ian hates organized religion, but he says, "I think it's nice. Maybe it will help." Then he turns to me and smiles. "Or maybe it won't."

Should I force myself anyway into the teeth of this, get him to talk about how maybe nothing will help? Alice would say I should. She says death should be greeted like a long-lost mother, something to be celebrated.

Maybe it's better to just go on, driving, driving, not having to arrive anywhere at all.

I say the light, easy thing: "You've covered all the possibilities." He laughs and then coughs, kneads his chest with his fingers.

The sun explodes over a rim of rock wall, and I think I see a wash of pink in the distance. We go around another bend, and suddenly the whole world is red. I'm sure of it. Stones wash down the hills, a high red tide of rock and sand. Crimson cliffs close in on the road, with curving folds like stage curtains, or enormous skirts.

"I wish Alice could be here," I say, suddenly sure that this is a moment we could agree on.

"Give it up," Ian says. "She shouldn't have kicked you out, not now."

This is the closest he's come to admitting that I might be needing someone's love. I glance at him, wondering if more should be said. But he's smiling, leaning forward to peer upward at the scarlet rim of rock. "This is beautiful," he says. "I wish my housemates could see." He pauses, adds, "And Susan. Did I ever tell you about Susan?"

I say, no, he hadn't, but he doesn't tell me, is evidently transfixed by the landscape. The skirts of red rock have come close to the road like old-fashioned mothers who would smother us against their aprons. The sky has become so intense I'm sure what I'm seeing is indigo blue, a color I've always wanted to know because I love the sound of the word: indigo. It's part of a family of wonderful-sounding words: staccato, amaretto, caterpillar, ambrosia.

We pass a sign saying *Arches National Park*. Alice made a fuss about Arches, but I'm hoping Mark's forgotten. More signs: motels, rafting outfits, a rock shop. We approach a bridge, a sign that seems to be a portent: *Colorado River.*

Ian says, "I need to take a leak." Just over the bridge is a little roadside park, and I pull off, find us the little potty huts. He unfolds his lanky body out of the wagon and walks carefully. I study the tall-limbed look of him, the gaunt stretch of his neck, which looks beautiful to me, his long swinging arms. It occurs to me that I'm memorizing him.

I get out of the car, walk down a path, press through a sticky stand of tamarisk to the edge of the river. We've come to the wide, muddy Colorado, the river that keeps the West alive. The swift current makes little circles in the water, rings floating, entwined like the Olympic insignia, then pulling apart, joining again. Maybe I'll write a song about how our lives are like those circles, joining and breaking apart, pushed along by deep currents and so on. If I'm equal to it, a song for Ian.

Ian comes toward me through the frothy tamarisk, wipes the sticky sap on his pants. His face is flushed, his eyes too bright. "I passed a little blood."

"Oh, oh."

"I suppose it's normal," he says. "I mean, for my condition."

"Should we find a doctor?"

"No. He'd keep me. I want to get to Houston."

We stand at the river's edge. The river tumbles thick and brown and swirling, and it's hard to believe what they say, that this river never makes it home to the ocean. So much is drained off for irrigation and hydro-electric power that it just peters out somewhere south of Death Valley.

"Mom died even younger," he says.

Mom curled on the sofa in the throes of her M.S., saying, "Your father doesn't love me." She was right, so what could we say? Once she took my hand and said, "You are full of feeling. It's wonderful," and I felt terrible, because she was wrong. All I felt around her was guilt and a great need to get away from her as fast as I could. When she finally died, I cried a little, but mostly because I felt bad for the lie I'd lived with her.

I say, "You've got a lot more to live for than Mom did."

"Yes, I do. And I will. Let's get going."

But he pauses, stays next to me staring at the water.

Then he starts making a funny sound like coughing, only deeper and drier. I've heard this sound only once before, which was that day his leukemia was discovered. I rushed up to him, worried that he was choking. "He's crying," one of his house mates said. "I heard it once before, when his father died. He cries funny."

I put my arm across his shoulders. He lays his head against mine for a moment, then pulls away, makes his sound apart from me. We stare at the circles, the moons of Jupiter, the center of flowers, breasts, boat shells, sand dollars, pennies for wishes, coins in the toll basket, ropes looped for the rappel, snakes coiling, mating, slithering away. I know it isn't the same as seeing color, but it's seeing shapes, and I think shapes have something to do with feelings, too.

"Let's go to Arches," he says.

"We passed it already."

"Alice says we should."

I feel Alice with us too much, bossy, wanting too much. "We've got a long way to get yet," I say.

"What's another hour?"

I don't say what, head the car away from the sun, spin us back a few miles. The ranger at the park gate collects the fee, hands us a map of the park, then asks, "Is one of you named Mark?" I say, "How'd you know?" He opens a drawer, fishes out a folded note, hands it to me. "Some lady phoned this in, said you'd be in an old maroon Volvo." I thank him, pull off to the side and read: *Knew you'd come here. I'm flying to Houston. Meet you at the clinic. Godspeed, Alice.*

It surprises me, the rush like agitated birds, the sudden swoop of fear and elation. Ian reads over my shoulder, says, "Now you'll have to marry her," which is exactly the thought that's crossed my mind.

I wind us up the steep narrow road into the park. The sand seems redder; the rock formations loom nearly on top of us, dark shape after incredible shape—towers, walls, human-shaped clusters—suffocating, closing in. I feel clobbered by too much heavy beauty. A sign tells us we've crossed the Moab Fault, and I wonder what if right now this fault slipped, split the ground wide open and swept us under. The landscape levels, seems normal, a soothing expanse of sand-colored mounds next to which is a sign: *Petrified Sand Dunes.*

Then, up into a new tangle of natural wonders. We pass Balanced Rock, which is another place where any minute something terrible could happen: the top-heavy boulder could thunder down, tossed by a blinded Cyclops. This makes me think of our father. I see the single-minded rage behind his silence, and I wonder if I'm afraid of being his kind of father.

A fork marked Windows leads us through a stretch of juniper and pinion. We come to Double Arch and park for a while, neither of us feeling energetic enough to get out and walk, though there's a trail and a sign warning us to stay off the cryptobiotic sand, which is alive with organisms built up over countless years. One footprint, you've destroyed an entire century.

Double Arch is an Escher-like giant pelvis, with a huge arch in front, another angling behind it, indigo sky in the middle. It's us, two brothers, circling each other, lots of space in between, but joined at the hip.

"Indigo blue." I say.

"Huh?" Ian laughs. "I think that's a very dark blue, an early night sky maybe."

I find this disappointing all out of proportion. Such a wonderful name ought to be right for this particular sky. Sometimes you have to be able to name a thing, like the actual color, the exact emotion. The arches look tenuous, unstable, and they are if you think in terms of eons, or if you stop to think that the moment of collapse probably comes in an instant.

Ian says, "Isn't there an Angel Arch somewhere?" He consults the map the Ranger gave us, can't find any Angel Arch. After a while Ian says, "I've seen enough. Let's go back." This fine with me. But when we return to the *Petrified Dunes* sign, he says he wants to stop and get out. Why here? This is the dullest stretch of the park—acres of low rippled domes that look like nothing.

But it's his trip, God knows. We get out and begin to walk. The mounds of petrified sand have a comforting, solid feel because the ripples give solid purchase to the feet. The air is unmoving, smells rich, gathered up, like the incense we used to burn when we smoked pot together, back when pot and so much else seemed harmless.

The frozen dunes dip into a steep gully, and I cry to Ian, absurdly, "Be careful! Don't fall!" Cupped in the base of the gully is a pothole filled with brilliant water, which might be what they call emerald green; when I walk closer it gets darker—Army drab? I suppose color is little more than the angle of the light, combined with the eye of the beholder—a great wonder—and I feel sad, thinking Ian and I have missed out on this range of possibility. A huge spider swims exactly in the middle of the pond, and bright dragonflies swoop around I wonder what becomes of them when the pothole dries up.

We climb up the other side of the gully, move across the expanse of rippled rock. My mind gears down, releases me from the road. I start to notice things: the silence, and then these amazing patches where the sand isn't petrified—artful circles like those miniature Japanese meditation gardens you create with little forks. Some master gardener has come along with, say, a twist of greasewood, a burst of sage, spread of prickly pear. Or two perfectly round black stones lie just so in a web of cryptobiotic sand. A late desert flower is silk from someone's fist. These gardens settle me, make me slow.

Ian has walked out ahead of me, all graceful angles and long loose limbs, a world-class climber even now. I stand and watch him, a mantis-man, a giant spirit-creature, a spider-limbed alien from some planet too benign for us to tolerate. He's found a cure. How could anyone walk so far ahead and not be cured? I'm feeling so strange, I even think it's all right if Alice prays for him. If she actually comes to Houston, is she forcing my hand? I feel like I'm tripping on acid, or writing, at long last, a really good song.

My brother strides and strides, giraffe-limber, dancer neck, arms loose like streamers. He could go on and on, straight into the sun, which pours out its heat now that it's higher. And he does go on and on, as if this is all he ever needed to do. He's way ahead of me. I kneel down, rub my fingers across the metallic gnarl of a dead juniper, let myself get lost in the possible color of silver. When I look up again, Ian is standing dead still like a tree washed bare by a sudden wind. He seems to be on the edge of something, and he's shouting.

I run, tripping over corrugations, wallowing in pits of sand, snagging in scraggles of brush. He's found a dead animal, perhaps, or a rattlesnake, or something worse. It's a long way to run. My brother Ian shimmers in the distance like a mirage, a waterfall, a pillar of light that any moment could vanish.

He's pointing to something on the ground, only that isn't exactly right either. What's stopped him is a canyon that drops maybe a hundred feet like a ragged earthquake fissure, a crevasse splitting a glacier. It's an astonishment, the falling away with no warning, the sudden end of everything.

He looks at me like a kid asking for permission. Be careful, I say, Ian, don't fall. We tiptoe to the very edge where we can see to the bottom. Way down, there's a trickle of a stream and an amazing abundance of green: tall cottonwoods, willows, fern-like plants hanging on the rock. From the road, you'd never imagine it possible. It's the Underworld in reverse. Up here almost everything is dead, mostly sand and rock. Down there is where the color is. Down there is where life seems to begin.

"Is this the place?" Ian says. He stoops in a sudden spasm of coughing, tries to hide it, but I see a streak of blood in his hand. He grins as if he's been caught at mischief. "Do you think I don't know?" he says. "I don't want to lie around that house waiting. We'll be in Houston together, maybe Alice, too; we'll be a family."

I catch hold of his arm, and he doesn't shake me off. Instead, he leans into me, and it's nice to feel the bones of him against me. Blood of my blood. My brother.

Under the Tornado

We were having a circle. It was Marlene's idea. She isn't shy about saying she's so lonely in this place she could die, and so she said, "Let's do like those churchy women here who have sewing circles, only let's do our art together." When we greeted this with silence, she said, "When I lived in Utah, I visited Taos and talked to an old Pueblo woman. She told me the women used to throw their pots together and gossip." Marlene is German, so it sounded funny when she said "throw their pots together" and we laughed. Marlene scowled and went on: "The old woman said that gossip was for them a circle of power."

"You sound like Shirley McClaine," Drew said. But Marlene is older than us, her German accent carries a certain authority, and we tend to listen to her even as we laugh. And so Marlene and Drew and Joy and I sat in the attic studio of Marlene's house, a little apart from each other at a long wide table, not really in a circle at all. The round skylight above us would have let in the sun, if there had been any sun. What came were the shadows of dark prairie clouds and a heavy yellow light that looked as if it smelled. Had it not been for the air-conditioner, the heat would've pressed us down in a heavy-handed way. No one was speaking. Perhaps it was the air or we'd forgotten the ancient art of gossip.

Sometimes Drew lets me watch her work. She sits in front of a mound of micaceous clay, her hands cupped around it like a pair of hips. Her eyes close as if she's waiting for something to come to her from inside the unformed mass. Then she's a whir of motion, reaching for a coil of wire, rushing outside for a bit of rock, a stick, a shard of glass, then back to the clay, tearing and poking things into it, pounding as if answering some frantic summons. And then, what she makes! It's beautiful and scary and strong.

Drew is a tamer of horses, a shaper of clay, the person I would most like to be.

I paint watercolors. I suppose they're good, or I wouldn't teach at the university here, but the colors wash like thin feelings and fade into each other as if nothing can make up its mind. It's kind of how George and I were together, blurry and pale, the boundaries unclear. Perhaps my paintings are good in the way that I am good as a person—too honest for my own good—and this isn't very interesting. I would like to be a lump of something. I would like to poke out rocks and sharp glass—not like Ian, who poked so hard he kept everyone in awe—but like a thing to be reckoned with, touched boldly, without fear.

At the end of the table sat Joy, humming and dabbing at one of her interminable peach-toned landscapes. Joy has lived here in central Illinois all her life. She's nearly as old as Marlene, but she has the mindless optimism of a child. She keeps herself alive by affirmations and the undying hope that she's a real artist. She took a class from me, but I couldn't help her very much, perhaps because what she paints is what I could end up doing if I'm not careful. But I like her. Underneath that dreadful cheerfulness is an interesting person. It's something I've learned to sense from being a teacher.

Marlene doesn't pretend to be an artist, but she loves to slap together huge collages, which are actually rather good. She collects things from wherever she goes and then does a collage about the place. She and Johann visit friends on the Oregon coast every summer, and spread before her were the things of that coast: some dried seaweed, a strip of bleached out wood, a flawed agate, a seagull feather, a clump of dried seagrass, and a mound of sand. I wondered how she'd get the sand to stick to the sheet of cardboard, which she'd been staring at for maybe thirty minutes. Marlene is the only one of us who's married. She has, unbelievably, been married to the same man for over twenty years. I wonder how she can stand that gruff old Teuton of a husband, but, who knows, underneath all that bluster could be a mensch and a gentle human being. They say it happens.

Drew hadn't gotten into her trance yet, and I couldn't seem to begin even a sketch. It was possible that our circle wasn't going to work. I wanted to do a place called City of Rocks where George and Ian and I climbed back in the days when our climbs were innocent and almost fun. The City of Rocks is a place in Idaho where great spires of granite rise up for miles like a Stonehenge gone mad. It may not be possible to make such a landscape seem real. I thought, for one thing, that I might be in the wrong medium. The problem, too, was I couldn't figure out which line in my memory had the power. I was obsessed with that time in my life: sharp crystals rasping into my knuckles, the harness pressing into my groin, the height so intense it would freeze me so I could go neither up nor down. George and Ian would wait silently, knowing I'd find a way to move around the fear. I was happy there with my two men: George, who loved me without reason; Ian, who believed in the best of me; for a while it was the finest life a person could imagine. I wanted to save it all, no line more important than the rest. Maybe that memory wasn't old enough for art. Maybe never will be.

I wish I were strong like Drew. I like to watch her ride her horse, Bill, she calls him, to see his muscles bunch like fists when he gathers himself for a jump and the little smile on her face and the blade of blunt-cut hair slicing in rhythm across her face. Drew is my closest friend, more so now that we are exiles from the place we love. It is by the sheerest of luck, if you can call it luck, that we both came here— she to follow Barry, me, to accomplish something, I don't quite remember what.

We tried to get Margaret to come down from Chicago for our circle, but she said she wasn't into art right then. Margaret may not be doing very well. Drew and I think Peter broke something inside her, and we don't know if it's something that can mend. She won't talk to us about it much. I have mending of my own to do, and I'm still trying to find a way to be strong. If I fail, I could end up like Lily, though I don't think I'm brave enough. Probably I'd be more like my mother, who became as vague and insubstantial as my most dreadful paintings.

Getting strong was why I learned to climb, did rugged, scary things; and when that wasn't enough, I divorced George and came here to be on my own. I can't remember what's so important about being on my own, though it's a thing people say you should want to do more than anything in the world. All that seems to come from living alone is the need for more and more time alone. You've chosen time alone, so it must have value; therefore, you hoard it, run your hands through all this time, all this silence, as if it's golden, like they always said. I love my silence—no radio, no TV—nothing but the hum of my own blood, waiting for the thought that will help me remember why I've done this. But when I am with others, silence seems to be an unbearable waste of our time together.

The yellow light breathing down through the skylight was getting thicker and it spoiled the colors, kept us apart. Everything seems kept apart in this strange part of the country, a place regulated and ordered, with not much forgiveness, not much love. Perhaps it's the implacable landscape that does this to people, a gray flatness that rules out certain memories of color, generosity and flow, forbids mad landscapes, magnificent disorder.

After a while Drew and Marlene and I gave up the pretense of work and laid down our props. We stared at each other and smiled, a little embarrassed, and waited for Joy to notice. Finally she felt our eyes. It was me she looked at. I'm usually the one she looks at when she talks. Perhaps she will never get over having been my student. "Susan," she said. "Why aren't you working?" She looked to the rest of us. "Is something wrong?"

Marlene rolled her eyes to the skylight. "Isn't that a tornado sky?"

Joy shrugged. "It's always tornado sky this time of year. I don't think about it." She dipped her brush in the tin of water, slathered it with lavender paint. She needed to be stopped. I didn't know why I thought this, but it came to me in a sudden rush of anger.

"What *do* you think about, Joy?" It was out of me before I could think how it sounded.

She stabbed her brush into the tin of water, stood up and stretched as if she'd just risen from a nap. "There could be a real tornado in that sky," she said.

If I had an umbrella, I'd have poked at her, don't know why. "So what do you think about?" I persisted. "You never talk about what you think."

"I think about birds."

Marlene leaned forward and said, "And what else?"

Joy looked around herself as if confused. "Well, what anyone thinks about. What to cook for dinner. What to plant in the garden."

Marlene sat back and looked tired. "My friends in Utah tried to plant a garden," she said softly, "but it failed, and because of that they bought a summer place on the Oregon coast and their marriage was saved, along with, probably, their lives."

Joy glared at her. She does not enjoy this sort of talk. Not many people do. Maybe that's why there's no power in gossip any longer; it's lost the real content, emptied of the real stuff of stories, the stories of our lives. For one thing, hardly anyone knows someone long enough. Such stories are now acceptable only on soap operas or in the therapist's office where they can challenge no one, change nothing.

Joy reminds me of the little girl my mother used to say I ought to be like. Besides not being able to love George, I did the only really mean thing I can remember to that little girl, smeared mud on her perfect dress, on her perfect curly hair, her sweet smiling face. I didn't want to be mean again. Can a person be strong without being mean?

Drew stood and started to walk around. "I can't get Barry to answer my calls," she said. "He owes me money."

"So hire a lawyer," Marlene said.

"I'm not ready."

"Don't wait," I told Drew. "You'll get cheated the way Margaret was."

"No way. Margaret was a fool about Peter."

"I think it's his kid she has the most trouble about," I said, "but I haven't talked to her for a while. Do you know how she's doing?" I asked.

"She doesn't belong in Chicago," Drew said.

"I wish you'd stop talking about people I don't know," Joy said and sat down, picked up her paintbrush and stabbed at a blob of paint. She'd ruin the brush that way.

"You don't know many people, I think," said Marlene. She stared up a while at the yellow coming through the skylight. "I miss the people who know me."

The sky seemed to make us heavy with our losses, with unfinished things, and there was anger edging our voices like strips of sheet metal. I wanted to smooth this over, which is another reason why I'm not strong. Anger has a way of evaporating the minute I know it's there, so there's never something to power me up.

We seemed unable to find a way back to each other. I thought I heard a siren, but it became part of the hum in my head, a hum that's grown louder the longer I live alone and then sit with others with whom I have nothing to say.

Joy leaped up and said, "I knew it! They've sighted a tornado."

Marlene slumped deeper into her chair. "Johann is applying for jobs back west. We have to get out of here. He was an idiot to take this job, even for more money."

"Wow," said Joy. "We could be in danger."

"Shouldn't we go to the basement?" Drew said. She picked at the lump of clay, rolled out little balls on the table, pushed them back into the lump.

"We don't have a basement." Marlene looked patient.

"Well, then, stand in a doorway, or something?" Drew walked the borders of the room, ready to go somewhere that had to be safer than there. I found this faintly disappointing. Of all of us, she should have been the least afraid. I felt, in contrast, rather strong.

Joy ran to the window. She was acting like a nervous child waiting for a visitor.

"I miss Barry," said Drew. "He'd know what to do."

"He would not," I said, the metal back into my tone. "Lily's the one who'd know. She's the one who should be with us."

"Who's Lily?" said Marlene.

Joy shrugged and smiled at her, "Who knows?"

Drew was silent a while, no doubt thinking of Lily, our friend, who'd dreamed of creating a community of artists in the desert and who has been dead for a few years. We hadn't spoken of her for a long time, and I didn't know why I'd thought of her just then.

Joy frowned at us from the window. "We need to watch. We need to hear if the siren keeps on going."

The yellow light overhead blacked out, like a burned-out lamp. Thunder and lightning cracked in the same instant, so loud and bright we jumped, and then the rain came in a stunning rush, beating on the roof in a sudden rage. I stepped over to Drew and touched her arm. Marlene was still slumped in her chair. It occurred to me for the first time that Marlene must have stories from her childhood in Germany that would make ours pale with insignificance.

Joy was leaping up and down and shouting. "The sky is incredible! Come look!" She turned to us from the window and her face was flushed with a passion I'd never seen. I walked through the thick air that made the room seem larger than it was, cupped my hands to the streaky glass, and saw a huge gray cloud drooping into the horizon like a great pregnant belly, the thing inside it kicking and heaving against the bulging clouds. It was more beautiful even than the ice-covered face of a mountain.

Drew peered over my shoulder and then shrank away. "We've got to figure out where to go," she said. "I think I'm getting an attack of vertigo." When no one spoke, she did a strange thing: she clambered up on the table, crawled around our stuff, and sat Indian-style directly under the skylight. Then she put her head in her hands and rocked a little. Then she looked up at us. "I still love him," she said. "I'm afraid of what will happen to me now."

I thought I should comfort her, but only briefly, for Joy's excitement had infected me. We were having the experience of a lifetime and I didn't want to waste any of it being afraid.

Marlene spoke from her chair. "I read something once about a woman who stood underneath a tornado and lived to talk about it." Drew and Joy and I turned our heads to Marlene, our mouths gaping open like children waiting to be read to.

This woman was about to climb into the trapdoor of a rootcellar, with little time to spare, for the tornado was close and dead on course. Her children, her husband, were already inside. Then she saw the tornado begin to rise, and she remembered that tornadoes sometimes skip and stay off the ground for long stretches. So she stood right where she was, and when the tornado skipped over her, she looked up, saw the inside.

A strange lethargy came over Marlene and she spoke slowly, paused. We waited for her to summon the energy to finish the story. A certain fullness of time seemed necessary. "It looked miles high," she went on at last. *It was black and louder than a hundred freight trains and smelled incredibly foul. It was full of lightning, all contained within it, streaking and bouncing like crazy pinballs trapped inside a chamber. Because of all that light, the woman could see trees and other things, God knows what, whirling inside it.*

Joy slapped her hand on the table. "Wow. I like the lightning part the best."

We were silent for a while, listened to the siren, which seemed to get louder.

Marlene stood and walked to the center of the room next to Drew. "I have an idea. Since we seem disinclined to save ourselves, let's sit underneath the skylight and see if the tornado skips over us. If it does, it's something we'll remember for the rest of our lives."

"It will most likely miss us altogether," I said, but no one seemed to hear me.

Joy clapped her hands. "It'll be sort of like a sea change. We'll never be the same again." She hurried to the wall, switched off the lights, drew the window curtains closed. "Let's do it right," she said. "Let's do it all."

I laughed, said, "There's no place like home."

"Maybe we'll find out where that is—finally." Marlene had set her jaw, looked quite Wagnerian.

Drew smiled at us from the table, and nodded. We climbed up on the sturdy table, shoving our stuff out of the way, and gathered ourselves in a tight circle underneath the skylight. We held hands. The silence became electric and brought back feelings I couldn't seem to use any more. Those feelings clustered like stubborn mountain flowers that grow out of cracks in the rock. Water knots. Ice, a glaze of fool's gold in the sunlight. Granite, the tough edge of the earth. The sounds of the person you used to live with.

"It's a seance," Joy said, like a joke, a buffer against the stories pressing into the air. But no one laughed, and after a few minutes, she whispered, "I wish I could call down Grace. "

We stared at her.

"My sister."

We didn't know she'd had a sister.

"I want to call her down," said Joy. "I want to tell her I'm sorry. I want her to teach me how to be an artist."

We waited. The siren kept on. Lightning seemed to strike not far away. We flinched, but held on and waited. The air in the room smelled of ozone and seemed thinner, as if we'd just finished a long, steep climb. The wind yammered like a pack of dogs.

Marlene made a sound that could have been a sob or a gasp. She was trembling. "I'm remembering things," she said. "It's all right. It had to happen sooner or later." She was silent a while and then, "I am ashamed."

"You were so young," Joy said, and reached across the circle to touch her knee.

"In certain times, like war, you look up, and the dark places are all lit up inside. You see things no human being should ever see."

The skylight swelled with a sudden brilliance and, just as suddenly, slid into darkness, a moon falling off the roof. We moved closer together, our restrained terror and excitement become forces that rocked us into the center until our heads touched, rocked us back out to look up and watch, and be—as we were, not yet knowing—inside the thing that could carry us home.

Angel's Landing

One morning on my way to work, dear Margaret, I had to walk around a pool of blood. I decided it was time to get out of New York and start my life over. This had to be accomplished in stages, beginning with a few small actions. I stopped trying to get Aunt Martha to approve of me. Didn't iron any more, for one thing, stopped sending her pretty flowered cards. She's a Midwesterner and likes to say, "Lily, you have to let Jesus into your heart."

She's right, by the way, though it's nothing like what she imagines. Nothing here is what you'd imagine either. The binary oppositions by which the brain organizes the world have no meaning here. No up or down, big or little. No ice, no fire. The contexts are gone, most notably one's body. What is here would be too much to handle inside a body, but I think it's a good idea to sample this kind of love before you die. Getting used to this place is like thawing out a frozen hand. It hurts in proportion to how badly you got frozen. And I was frozen to the bone. Now I'm fine, but I'm sorry I died when you needed me. I want to tell you some of my beforelife in the hopes that it will help.

I tried making lists in order to know myself. I thought it might be good to make a list I titled: WHAT A REAL WOMAN IS LIKE. I began with the bottom line: "Not like a man, i.e. not as many red corpuscles." I couldn't seem to get out from under the tyranny of parallel structure, so each item began with the word "Not," and the list came out as if men were the sky and the rest of us were visible only in relief against that sky, like mountains in the darkness.

Then I made a list of all the men I'd slept with. Those whose names I couldn't remember, I wrote down what they did for a living, which seemed more important at the time. Jack Something, trumpet player and skydiver, was still in my life then. He had little knobs on the tops of his shoulders, which I'd gotten used to. The trial lawyer was also in my life then. He had a breastbone like the prow of a ship. I never got comfortable with him. This was during the sexual revolution, a sad time in history when men and women got naked in a frenzy of hope that this time it could mean something. This is another list I tore up.

Dear Margaret, I never tore up your letter, please be assured of that. I am a long time in answering. I'm sorry. Though you haven't written again, I'm in a position to know what's happened since you wrote. I know that Peter asked you to leave him and Robert, whom you love as your own child, and that you're now living with a cousin in Chicago. I know you think it's your fault. You think you've run out of time. As you can imagine, this is something I identify with, and I want to tell you the rest of my story even though some of it you already know.

I bought clothes for all the women I might become: tailored-tweed woman, neo-hippie India print natural woman, ruffly feminine complete with lipstick, mountain-desert outdoorswoman. The options made me dizzy. I had so many clothes there wasn't room for them in my closet. Finally, I gave most of them away, except the outdoors stuff and a few feminine things, just in case.

Jack, the trumpet player, invited me to skydive with him. I said yes, of course. I was game for anything, but by then I was thick into planning my escape from New York and didn't have any more time for him.

I sold my furniture and my beat-up piano which I hadn't played for years anyhow. I don't know why, but in that city I couldn't handle making music. My reach had become too small, I think because my hands were too often curled into fists. And I didn't feel safe enough to open that space inside me from which the music must come. You know what I'm talking about. I'm talking about the space carved out long ago like a river channel, a honeycomb in the sandstone, a clean, empty cup into which would someday flow the love of a human being (or, who knows, even the love of Jesus) and out of which could then pour my secrets and a heart brimming with stored-up love. This is, dear Margaret, the essence of hope and the place where the splendid fiction of time is kept alive.

I did manage to write a little poetry and discovered a certain flair. It's a lot like composing music: you lift up a handful of sounds into the sunlight and toss them like seeds onto the desert. A few of them take root, find a little water and explode into cactus thorns, a little blood, then into flowers, the petals falling into patterns, motifs and themes, one flower much like the next, elaborations, increments. If the seeds are good, almost anything is possible by this method.

Even so, it became clear that I'd have to do something drastic to extricate myself from New York, which anyone will tell you is nearly impossible. So I signed up for an Outward Bound course in the Utah desert. The trial lawyer told me how I could make some "escape money" by getting myself hurt, say breaking a leg on one of the climbs, and then suing them. I didn't even consider it, which made me feel good about myself. Shreds of morality I clung to, though I don't think anyone would have cared either way, not even Aunt Martha.

One of the first things we did on Outward Bound was to walk across a log suspended over the Virgin River. The weight of my backpack pulled me off balance, and into the water I went, soaking everything. I twisted my ankle, but I didn't think this was worth writing to the trial lawyer about. I walked so slowly that the others on the patrol soon hated me. I almost didn't mind, for we hiked where the redrock canyons close around you like a birth canal and the darkness falls so suddenly you think you've lost your memory at last.

Like the men on my list, I can't remember the names of the men on my patrol, except for two nicknames: Motor Mouth and Gibbons. Motor Mouth had just come out of the Marines and this apparently qualified him to sputter an unending stream of words ranging from "cunt," to "prick," varied by spurts of, "Press onward!" Gibbons, a landscape artist, was, by contrast, the kind of man you could start over with. He would hike alongside sometimes and say encouraging words, share his water, smile sympathetically at my limp. The other woman on the patrol was Kate Something. I needed us to be sisters, but her eyes slid away from mine, and she wouldn't talk much to me, even in the darkness by the fire. This bothered me for a long time after, for it was a failure on my part to form what should be a basic sort of bond. What seemed to come easily to others mystified me. It felt as if someone had left out an item or two in the list of instructions entitled: HOW TO BE A MEMBER OF THE HUMAN RACE. The things I did over and over were not incremental like petals on a flower, but grew out crooked and bent back into me like an ingrown toenail. Because I was an intelligent person, I could watch and imitate and pass for human. But beneath all that, way down in the part of ourselves we save, was that being I can now, despite my obvious failures, call a real woman.

We hiked across more rivers, over vast mounds of slickrock, threaded our way through juniper and cedar and sage, yucca and prickly pear, canyons so narrow we had to squeeze, sand dunes so thick we wallowed and sank. We roped up, roped down, leaping off cliffs like spiders. We got thirsty, smelly, bone tired, blood-red hot, freezing cold at night. I limped along under my pack and asked myself every hour or so: have I started my life over yet?

I wrote letters by the light of the campfire, but I did not write to my father. For the first time in my life, I did not write to him. Unless you know the whole story, you can't realize what a step that was.

My poems began to bleed into stories, which my father would never see. I thought about going back to college.

Jack sent me a letter saying, "Outward Bound will make you a better person." Was it so obvious that I needed to be a better person? Who was he, anyway? But in my sleeping bag under the cold stars I thought of the knobs on his shoulders and those skydiving arms. And I thought of my father, who also told me I should become a better person while he fumbled for my breasts after Mother had gone to bed. His eyes were innocent and round and very sad.

Our patrol climbed Angel's Landing, a monolith of sheer sandstone, terror. From the top, you could see mile after mile of red rock jutting up from the earth like flares of temper. You could slice yourself open diving into that sharp blue air. At that very moment, perhaps, Jack was leaping into the same sky a couple thousand miles away. I wanted overwhelmingly to dive, yet I clung to the rock as if it were my mother, or the mother I wished I'd had.

I began writing letters to my mother. Never mind that she'd already died. You'll understand this, having written a letter to me like that. I can tell you now, the effort isn't wasted. I told my mother that when she was dying I'd finally noticed the beautiful bones in her face. I told her that I saw sense now in the things she used to say, like, "Stand up straight," or "Don't climb all over your father." I assured her that she was a far more interesting woman than her sister Martha, and I told her about being in Outward Bound, because I thought she'd like to know I could be sort of brave.

My ankle healed and I finally got into in my stride, clumping my boots into the sand like somebody who could make a dent in things. Except for Gibbons, the guys on the patrol said I'd been faking it all along, especially when it turned out I was pretty good at rock climbing. I watched the muscles come out on my legs: the long-suppressed secret of a strong body.

Another letter from Jack. He said he'd done a six-pointed star but was having some trouble with his *embouchure*. He hoped I was planning to come back to the city for good. I was tempted. Jack understood things about me, like why I'd stopped playing piano and why sometimes a person wants to dive into the sky.

They left us alone for three days, strung a mile apart from one another along a vast bluff of Navajo sandstone where seeps could be found at the base of the rock. They gave each of us a cup, a tarp, and a few matches. No sleeping bag, no food. I was tired and clumsy, spilled water on my matches and had no fire against the bitter night cold. I tried to keep warm by burying myself in the sand, thought of that Japanese art film, *Woman in the Dunes*, where for almost two hours you watch a woman sinking helplessly into the sand. In the morning I crept out of my hole, sand in my hair, my mouth, and burning like salt on the back of my neck. I sprawled on a little hill, letting the sun warm me. Toward noon I crawled under a juniper and thought about rattlesnakes, which also sleep under junipers. I was too tired to be afraid. I thought of them instead as sweet sisters and brothers under the skin, entitled to a little shade like anybody else, and I slept some more.

And then another night. "Daddy," I cried out, when I was so cold. I am ashamed of this. I never got over wanting him to love me.

Seeps are the miracles of the desert. They are created by snowmelt percolating deep into rock. All summer long the rock cradles this water, giving it back to the desert a few trickles at a time. At the base of a seep I held out my cup to the water, stumbled back to the shade, thought about the self-control of rock that did not gulp water all at once like sand, but had saved it for me, as if I were, in truth, someone worth saving.

Hummingbirds hovered around me, perhaps because my shirt was red. I got my period, and for three days I was a solitary red flower, blood on the sand, another baby that never got off the ground.

When I was reunited with the patrol after the solo, I no longer minded Motor Mouth nor did I dream of starting my life over with Gibbons. Weightless as a red-tailed hawk, I felt I might never need another person again.

Kate got burned on her shoulder from the Big Rappel, but she never complained, which made me feel guilty about having talked about my ankle. The pack strap must have hurt horribly. Only once could I get her to talk with me. The way she cast her eyes about as she spoke of her man back home told me he didn't love her very much. Perhaps women who do things like Outward Bound aren't loved and think they have to prove they're made of something better than lists of men or groceries, or whatever.

And then it was over, with hardly a backward glance from my patrol-mates, with whom I'd failed to form even the most rudimentary bond except for Gibbons, who was kind to everyone. I went straight to a hotel and ate two steaks and three servings of ice-cream. I slept for three nights and the better part of three days. I took countless showers, scalding baths, and stood naked in front of the full-length mirror, marveling at my body, as honed down and perfect as it would ever be.

I didn't tell my Aunt Martha I was stopping in the Midwest on my way back to New York, but I did visit my father. Feeling strong enough at last to do this, I sat him down, looked into his sad face and said: "What you did was wrong. You should have been a father to me. I love you, but not like that. Never like that." He pretended at first not to know what I was talking about, made those round eyes that had gotten him everything in life. When I said again, "You were wrong." his eyes became narrow and sly and he tried to twist my words, to blame, and, failing that, to put his hand on my thigh. I told him that this made me wish I were dead, and was that what he wanted, that I be dead? He said, "Come on, come on, you know you want me," and touched me again. The space I'd kept open and waiting behind my ribs froze itself shut, and I knew I'd never get to love anyone the way a person should.

I wrote a letter to my mother, telling her about him and me. I figured she was in a position to handle it now. I got to cry a little, imagining her smiling sadly and saying, "I knew it all along. I was afraid of him. I'm so sorry." And then, no longer needing her to be contrite, I heard her say, "There, there, my darling, it's all right." This felt very sweet and sad, but it was somehow not enough, and I began to see that I'd nearly used up my allotment of time, so I hurried back to New York, the faster to get out of there.

Jack couldn't handle the way I'd muscled up and my endless talk of handholds, water knots, and seeps. Never mind the skydiving ploy, he'd liked me as a fragile city flower. I got to cry a little about this, too, and then feel free to make my plans. I didn't feel like calling the trial lawyer.

It is strange and exhilarating to make plans for your life when it's already over. Is this what you're thinking now, that your life is over? I can understand why you'd think that, but I can see inside you a carved-out hope wider than the Great Basin. I tell you, that's what keeps a person alive, and you're kept alive, like it or not.

As for me, the rest you know: I made it out of New York, went to grad school, studied under Peter, wrote some good stories, got back into the piano for a while, loved you, enjoyed a few more men. I climbed some mountains with Susan, rode horses with Drew, camped in the desert, fell into a couple more rivers. The desert is a holy place. It is more holy, even, than Bach. I think of my time in the west as the years I stole. And what years they were!

I tried to prepare you for the fact that I wasn't going to make it. But you can't say to someone, "I've nearly used up my time." So I invented, dear Margaret, my obsession with planning a desert community, where we kindred spirits would someday live in adobe houses, throw pots and smudge each other with sage smoke. No harm, was it? You got to imagine a graceful way to get the leap on Peter, who from the start didn't love you, and I got to pretend I was still living in a world full of time. I couldn't stand watching you try and try and try with Peter. I wanted to drag you up Angel's Landing and push you off and say, "Fly, you beautiful woman, fly!"

But even now I lack the certainty I preach. Maybe I should have gone soft again and stayed with Jack. Or maybe the trial lawyer could have made me rich and then people would have read my stories and I wouldn't have been left alone in the desert and wouldn't have tried to talk to my father. There are other ways this story could have gone, unless you believe in predestination——which I kind of do, actually—a notion I might have picked up from Aunt Martha and possibly the reason it seemed inevitable that I should die by what they call my own hand.

I know my death puzzles you because I was someone people called "full of life." All I can tell you is that the idea of killing myself was with me ever since I can remember. It was what I had to do someday, a duty almost, as if someone had whispered a command into my ear while I slept. So I had to fill every minute with beauty and adventure until my time ran out.

As I read over what I've written here, I see moments where my logic might have been a little shaky. It is possible, for instance, that I was wrong about predestination and also wrong about time. Perhaps what was whispered while I slept was a lie, and if I could have bought some more time, I might have learned that. I know for certain I was wrong when I told you that we were women who couldn't live alone inside our bodies. The popular books that insist that this is something we ought to accomplish are also wrong. What I know now is that we're never alone, but our bodies fool us into thinking that we are.

You, as I've said, have a great deal of time, but you don't have time to live someplace you don't love. What are you doing? Chicago is a place like New York, where you can get caught. At least Susan and Drew live where nothing stays for long, not even the birds. Did you know that central Illinois is a flyway? Very few birds nest there; they just swoop down on their way north or south to catch a few of those heartland flies. You should have stayed in the west, in the sharp blue air that cuts your losses with love so incisive, so impersonal, you feel almost clean again.

So maybe I should have stayed in the west, too, ha ha. But if I had, Peter would have come on to me after he sent you away, and I wouldn't have known how to refuse him. He was, after all, my teacher, and I was hopeless when it came to saying no. That man knows his way around the women. You couldn't have saved either of us, even if you hadn't made mistakes.

I don't know if anything here might help, but I wanted you to know I'm still around, so to speak. Just please, whatever you do, don't try to call me down in a seance. I'm in a good place, but it's still a little tenuous.

I never stopped liking men, isn't it odd? I enjoyed those stolen years enormously. Which reminds me of another way I stole some time: I learned to think positively. Never say, "It's a shame she died so young." Instead, try: "Look how long she got to live, and how splendidly." You have to look on the bright side of things.

And so, in closing I give you that thought, abused as it is by people who use cheer to brush aside your pain. And one more thing: should you decide to take up writing or some other sharp blue leap into the sky, I give you Angel's Landing. And I give you my cup and the saving water of seeps.

Six Things That Keep Me Alive

1. My job in a doctor's office. Just barely.

2. The crab apple tree in my neighbor's courtyard, an astonishment in this sprawl of cement.

3. My dog, a scrawny brown thing with a widow's peak and gentle anxious eyes. She found me weeping with the gulls atop a blocky jumble of Lake Michigan shoreline.

4. The rocks I brought with me from Utah. Among them are some geodes I found near Dugway Proving Grounds, which is where they test biological agents and nerve gas.

5. E-mails from Susan and Drew. They, too, have been forced to migrate to Illinois. All three of us, for different reasons. Almost everyone I know is in exile one way or another.

6. My writing. Every night I talk metaphors to a blank page, and they tell me what I'm thinking.

The temp agency said I was lucky to get this job, I'm so overqualified.

In the tree is an empty nest. A best childhood memory: robins feeding their babies in the crook of our drainpipe. My mother, who was not yet ill, called me to the window to watch them.

This dog was suddenly there, speaking in worried little howls. Around her neck was a collar, horribly tight. No tags, hipbones jutting out, sores on her ears.

In a dark blue bowl, like fallen stars, lie the quarz crystals I found on my mountain hikes with Robert. When he began to call me "Mom," I tried to tone down the surge of elation, didn't want to push.

Sometimes I feel like a baby bird, a gaping maw of too much wanting.

I had no idea what to do with this dog, so I loosened her collar, which otherwise might soon have choked her, tied my scarf to it, and led her to my two-room apartment I'd just moved into. Next day to the vet, the rabies shot which registered her as legally mine. This contract is for life.

It came to me one day in front of the lions and Robert took my hand for the first time: Love is what you decide to keep doing--or not. Peter decided not.

My step cousin, Liz, let me stay with her until I found a job and a place to live. I am grateful, but we are neither kin nor kindred. She has a gorgeous doberman who is, to her owner's delight, both friendly and frightening. Liz says she hates intellectuals, says it over and over as if it's a message that could save my life.

Dr. Green is a dermatologist and books eighty patients a day, so I was surprised he had no clue how I might treat Lucy's ears.

I was weeping out of habit, and because of the whitecaps on the lake. Now, with this dog around, I can't indulge myself, because it makes her cry, too. I've named her Lucy, maybe thinking of a sky with diamonds, or the indelible media icon we're compelled to add: I Love.

144

My most prized treasure is an arc of white agate curved like a swanboat. Lily found it on our hike out to Delicate Arch. After her suicide, we found it holding down a note that said: "Margaret, I want you to have this."

Are there robins in Chicago?

Drew e-mails me that central Illinois is a flyway, which means that birds migrate through, don't stay for long. Susan, she says, hates the place, too, but loves teaching at the university. Is that what Liz means-- that being an intellectual keeps a person in the wrong place?

Water suspended in the silica is why these rocks look as if they are alive. The ancients said they carried spirits inside.

Big mistake not keeping him as my professor, who, as such, was without peer.

Robert was trying to make sense of why his mother left him, and now he must wonder why his stepmother is also gone. No matter how carefully you explain, kids blame themselves.

Chicago, as cities go, is rather nice. The neighborhood stores are the way I imagine they once were in small towns. You don't get lost in these stores. You get to know the owners. Some of them have dogs sleeping in the doorways.

My neighbor sometimes comes out and sits on the white bench under his crab apple. He waves to me. His hair is the color of Navajo sandstone.

Dr. Green, a skin-deep sort of man, treats me as if I'm invisible. I've gained a little weight and am no longer viewed as a pretty woman. Interesting. Unsettling. A brand new way of being (or not being) in the world.

My job, and everything else, is temporary, even the lake, though it seems to go on forever. I think a person needs to keep some illusions.

And I think this is why I write: to keep alive everyone and everything I've known, and to keep on believing that such a thing is possible.

And I think the stuff we hold up to the sun as the most important-- being loved, having a family, prestige, all that--isn't a reliable measure of a life. Too much is impossible to control. You can't count on what other people decide (or don't decide) to do. What I've come to trust is what I can do, the little stuff, like remembering to carry a plastic bag when I take Lucy for a walk.

Lily was a brilliant pianist and writer, also our good and passionate friend. Susan and Drew and I try to understand why she did it, and to honor, instead of resist, her choice. It was, for one, something she could do.

Lucy tore down my mini-blinds the first time I left her alone. Something a dog can do, which I hadn't had the foresight to imagine. Separation anxiety, it's called. Ah.

The tree is filled with hopeful little flower faces. Any one of them might produce a tree. They wait for bees, get to tremble, spew out some pollen, flutter. Nature is lavish with her foreplay.

I have a hunk of petrified wood streaked though with yellow, orange, and pink. It's so beautiful I can hardly stand to look at it. This is another proof that I am, as men are fond of saying, too sensitive. For what, exactly?

I was crazy about sex. Was that the problem?

My poems can't make me visible again, not even the published ones. I couldn't see it then, would have laughed at such a thought, but I

146

existed through the turning of heads. That is to say, others told me I was really there. It's the old tree-in-the forest question now.

A young woman in the waiting room: her face is covered with weeping sores. She tries to hide behind her hair.

Today the tree is mobbed with starlings. They clatter like one of those old tractor-feed printers and scatter petals like crumpled paper. These birds were brought to America by some misguided intellectual who thought every bird named by Shakespeare had to live in the New World. As exiles, they are horrible. Perhaps in England, they had better manners.

I've devised a parting ritual for Lucy: a treat in a box she can tear up to whatever extent her anxious heart requires. Now she loves it when I leave.

My neighbor comes into his courtyard, and the starlings fling skyward, thank God. He smiles at me and waves, sits down on his white bench, and pulls out a sheaf of papers and a pen. The fence between us is chain link. Not pretty, but it lets me see outside the desiccated patch of weeds behind my apartment.

Dr. Green dictates routine letters in addition to his turgid medical reports. I politely remind him that I have a Master's in English and will happily compose those letters, but he won't hear of it. Dictating must make him feel important.

Drew and Susan keep begging me to visit them. I can't, not yet. I've wrapped Chicago around me like a shabby blanket. Sometimes when you're cold, it's best to huddle and wait.

I used to take Robert on hikes in the mountains, or to the zoo, or to the Aviary in Liberty Park. I had this notion that if he could learn to appreciate birds, he'd be all right.

Inside the geodes are curving bands of agate and some crystals. Why, in the face of this, must they make nerve gas? I can't bend my mind around this one. Men in power seem to think it makes them indestructible if they can kill everything else.

The deli owner has an aging German Shepard who merely opens one eye when you step over him, closes it again. This deli carries Landjager, a wickedly delicious sausage. The owner lets me bring Lucy inside, and this helps me see another great divide between Europe and America.

Lucy runs to the fence, talking in her urgent way with funny little howls. This time he offers his hand for her to lick through the links. He tells me his name is Don. Thus, Lucy provides the proper introduction which my mother said you need before you speak to a man.

The doberman fixes you with stares like a cat and will eat nothing but fried steak and rice. Sometimes Liz and I walk our dogs together, though it's a little tense. I love Liz. We grew up together, after all. She is supremely confident and enjoys being an angry woman. I tend to be a sad woman, find myself closing down around her like a daylily at night. That gets old, too. Both of us, we work at being happy, believe in the idea.

I mean, some of it was my fault, of course. I see, for instance, that I was way too eager with him. You can't play tennis all by yourself. Me, I kept leaping over the net, trying to demonstrate how to do love. Come on, I kept calling out, play with me, it's fun!

I watch a lunar eclipse over the lake, and clutch at the obvious: dark times are nothing more than temporary shadows. Lately, I find myself in the middle of every truism I despised in my childhood. Now I let them comfort me, and see that they are, well, true.

The blossoms are falling open like tiny books. The nest still waits.

The starlings have evidently decided to dump their anger somewhere else, thank God.

Don comes outside more often now, it seems, and he's begun to give Lucy bone-shaped biscuits he must have bought just for her. We talk through the fence, our fingers clawed into the links like raptors. He's a high school science teacher and speaks with great excitement about how, say, a kid finally got turned on by the properties of sulphur.

I pick Lucy up at the vet after work. Spay time, a no-brainer decision, though it reminds me I never had a child, not from my body. Peter believed that omission disqualified me as a good mother for Robert. He actually said that. Everything I was taught about being a woman tells me I've failed, which frees up a strange exhilaration.

My mother died at fifty. Soon I will outlive her, and that will be a betrayal of sorts, as well as another brand-new freedom.

How does it get to be all right for us (but no one else) to make deadly germs? Don and I start to go at this through the fence, end up buying corned beefs at the deli and walking with Lucy to the lake. We munch, lick Dijon off our fingers, and speak our worries for America. We sound like fretting parents who see their uncontrollable child lurching toward disaster. It's clear that we love this child, rather passionately, in truth. Love is not the same as letting someone do whatever he wants. It's much harder than that.

Lily had three abortions. No matter your politics, this is a great sadness, but her choice was a mercy. Lily knew she couldn't keep a child alive, let alone herself. Oh, but the stories she birthed! The woman was a genius. This world overshadows such a gift. I hope there's a clear, bright place for the likes of her.

I send Robert cards, little gifts. I sent him a poem about the nest in the tree, which I now worry might make him sad. He courted me more than Peter did, kept telling me he loved me, drew stunning pictures of birds, things a gifted four-year-old could do.

The young woman ties back her hair now. It turns out she's rather pretty. Despite himself, Dr. Green is a healer.

Don has a habit of messing up his hair with his fingers, letting the longish strands go every which way. I think he's a few years younger than I. I've let my hair grow out. Pure white does sudden streaks from each temple, a thing you can't prepare for. But it's possible that these shocks of pale are, well, pretty.

If I'd expected less, would he have kept me? Or if I'd demanded more? Did I really want to be kept? Robert confused the issue so.

Sometimes the lake fades into mist, and the seagulls are strangely subdued so you can hear the slaps of the water against the rocks. Don and I find ourselves whispering when it's like this. Lucy lowers her head, stretches from tip to tail, and I see how beautiful she's become.

He says he'd like to see my rock collection. Are we talking etchings here? But no. Or not exactly. I think he's a friend, something new in a life where men had no time for friendship. And I'm no longer what they used to call irresistible. Thank God.

I seem to be saying that a lot lately. It's just a manner of speaking, of course. I stopped going to church as soon as I got out from under my parents. Maybe I'll begin trying to talk to God, but not like they thought I should.

I hold up the petrified wood, gushing, as is my wont, over its glorious array of color. Don cups his hand over my hair, barely touching. Nothing more. Birds rise in my chest. Is there still time for the wind to gather, the whitecaps to enter the dance, slowly, slowly? It terrifies me that I might find out I can't be with a truly kind man. Or that I will choose wrong again under a different guise. Or will choose well, for once. In truth, I've begun to enjoy these wide rocking waters, and myself amazingly afloat, contained only by a jumble of rocks and a skyline and the joyful cries of a dog.

Lily is walking around my mind a lot these days. She stoops to stroke a silver gleam of greasewood, smiles up at me, and says, "There's a seventh thing you haven't put a name to yet, a seventh thing that keeps you breathing in and breathing out. It isn't at all like you think. You'll be astonished."

Printed in the United States
27821LVS00001B/172

9 781893 239388